THE
NIGHT
CHILD

Center Point
Large Print

**This Large Print Book carries the
Seal of Approval of N.A.V.H.**

THE NIGHT CHILD

ANNA QUINN

CENTER POINT LARGE PRINT
THORNDIKE, MAINE

This Center Point Large Print edition
is published in the year 2018 by arrangement with
Blackstone Publishing.

The text of this Large Print edition is unabridged.
In other aspects, this book may vary
from the original edition.
Printed in the United States of America
on permanent paper.
Set in 16-point Times New Roman type.

ISBN: 978-1-68324-740-1

Library of Congress Cataloging-in-Publication Data

The Library of Congress has cataloged record
under LCCN: 2018001974

*For all the children
waiting for us to save them.*

CHAPTER ONE
NOVEMBER 27, 1996

Nora glances at the clock above the classroom door. Thirteen minutes until she will retreat with her husband and daughter to the Washington Coast. Every Thanksgiving since she and Paul have been married, fifteen years now, they've rented a room at the Kalaloch Lodge, a 1930s inn standing on a bluff above the rocky shore. Though it's only a few hours from Seattle, it feels as if they're visiting a distant relative, and it's better than sitting together, alone in the city.

"This book has no plot, no conflict," mumbles Jason, a sixteen-year-old underachiever who surprised everyone, including himself, when he passed the AP English test and secured a place in Nora's class. Now it's her job to get him into an Ivy League school—God, the way his mother hovers and pushes!

"You're an idiot," Elizabeth says to him. Gorgeous, brilliant Elizabeth, the girl who does everything possible to disturb. The girl who smears black around her eyes, dyes her hair an unnatural obsidian, and cuts it into angry asymmetrical lengths that hang over half her face.

They are discussing Woolf's *To the Lighthouse*,

and they are distracted—impatient for the week-long break. "What do the rest of you think?" Nora asks in an unusually quiet voice, walking between the rows of desks. She knows she should say more—she loves this book. She wants to discuss daring writers—how they sometimes veer off traditional plot trajectories, that not every story has a beginning, middle, and end, and yes, Jason, there is conflict! Look at the power the father exerts over the son, the need of the mother to keep her son a child forever, how badly Lily wants to paint. There's so much Nora wants to say, so much she wants to ask them, but a headache is growing from the base of her skull, like someone piling stones in her mind, flattening her thoughts, weighing her down.

"Plot means action," Jason says.

"God, the action's in their heads, you cretin," Elizabeth says, drawing skulls on the cover of her notebook and darkening the eye sockets, her fingers thin as pencils, her nails bitten to the quick, the stubs of them painted pitch black.

"No wonder she killed herself," Jason says with a smirk.

Darkness falls across Elizabeth's face then, but before Nora can say anything, the bell rings, the bodies bolt out the door, and Elizabeth is gone.

Nora walks slowly to her desk and collapses into her chair. She looks at the empty desks. "I don't know any of you," she says, wearily. She used to be energized by teaching, awakened and alive, used to go home and say, "How did I get so lucky, that this is what I get to do?" She used to allow students to write what they wanted, what they needed to, recommended books to them, offered options until their faces opened and their defenses dropped. But now, so many kids crammed in a small space, so many government requirements and ulterior motives—she has grown depleted and a bit hopeless.

It happens then.

A subtle movement of air behind her. More than a quiver of wind, more like someone exhaling. She turns around quickly. No one. But again, in front of her, another whisper. Her skin tightens and a chill shoots through her. She turns around. No one. Another movement. "What is it?" she says, aloud.

Oh, God. Panic tightens her chest and chokes her breathing. In front of her, a girl's face, a wild numinous face with startling blue eyes, a face floating on top of shapeless drapes of purples and blues where arms and legs should have been. Their eyes meet and terror rushes through Nora's body—the kind of raw terror you feel when there's no way out, when every cell in your body, your entire body, is on fire—when you think you might die.

A moment later, the face is gone.

Nora sits for a few moments, heart beating fast,

still in its grip. *What the hell was that? Did some little asshole put something in my coffee? Am I so tired I'm hallucinating? Shit.*

She takes deep breaths, rubs her eyes hard with the heels of her hands, and stares at the place where the face had floated moments ago. Nothing. Nothing is there any longer. The face has gone. *Okay then. You are fine now. You are fine. You just need rest, that's all. Just some rest.*

A man's voice behind her says, "Ready for the break?"

She turns around, blood still pounding in her ears. "John," she says, her voice a whisper. John in his slouchy tweed blazer, his hands plunged into his jean pockets as if he were just a teacher killing time between classes, not the principal of Lincoln High. The strength and warmth of him as he leans against the doorframe. The broad set of his shoulders, the ease of his grin, touch her and, in this moment, calm her racing heart.

"You okay?" he asks, closing the door and walking into the room.

She blinks fast, tries to blink away the blue eyes still bright at the edge of her mind. For a moment she considers telling him, telling him what happened—they've been friends for so long. She considers telling him, but her mouth doesn't feel right, doesn't feel like it can move enough to describe what she saw, but she tries to speak anyway, though only two words, *"I'm fine,"* come out and the words seem muffled, seem far away, not her voice at all, and she doesn't attempt to say more. She stands then, even though her legs tremble and for a second she holds onto the desk and John reaches for her with both hands, clutches her arms, asks her again if she's okay and she says again that she's fine, just tired, and she smiles a little to reassure him. He drops his hands when she reaches for her coat on the back of the chair. She pulls her coat on, buttons it slowly, watches her fingers push each black button into its hole, aware her fingers don't feel like they belong to her at all. And now, his hand touching her arm again.

"Nora," he says. "What is it?"

She wants to say something but she can't, and she plucks up her book bag and rushes out of the classroom and down the orange-tiled hallway and out the front door. The cold November air like a slap. She stops. Draws in the cold air deep, and it's the cold air, the startling sharpness of it, the white puffs from her mouth, that begin to anchor her to the present. *Thank God.* She doesn't want to have to explain to Paul what happened—he would only worry, might use it as a reason to stay home rather than travel. He is not one to relax all day long, let alone an entire week.

"Nora! Nora! Over here!" Paul shouts from the rolled-down window of his black Saab.

She walks, speeds up her pace, wants to appear

11

normal, speeds toward him, speeds toward the concrete noun of him, so real and specific in his black car, the car reorienting her even more, and the shock of what happened has almost completely subsided now, though she can still feel the residual fear of it, a light dusting of it throughout her entire body.

"Just your imagination," she whispers, her mouth working better now, and by the time she opens the car door and slides in, she feels almost completely normal.

"You okay?" Paul starts the engine. It's started to drizzle, and he flips on the windshield wipers.

"Yeah." She drops her book bag on the floor between her legs.

"Hi Mommy!" Fiona shouts from the back seat. "Are you excited to go on our trip?"

Nora takes one more deep breath and turns toward Fiona with a smile. Her daughter's small freckled face flushed with excitement, her arms wrapped around a stuffed orca. "Absolutely," Nora says, clicking her seatbelt. "Absolutely."

CHAPTER TWO
NOVEMBER 28, 1996

In the hotel, Nora pulls open the heavy curtains and is immediately comforted by the wide expanse of beach, water, and sky. The tide plunges in, silver-colored water flashing whitecaps like a thousand gulls who might at any moment lift up to the sky, light meeting light. Fiona, already on the beach, happy to be alive, laughing and chasing a white feather, her blonde hair flying wild. Paul strides behind her, hands in his pockets. He moves differently here than he does at home. Here, in the beach grasses, he is easier, but at home, when she sits with him at the kitchen table, the purple lupines in a vase between them, his tranquility vanishes behind his preoccupations and she feels an overwhelming urge to knock the vase over.

Lately, the way he is makes her (and Fiona too, Nora can see it on her face) feel unnecessary and alone. Fiona often asks her why Daddy is so busy, but Nora's explanation is nebulous, and she'll say, "It's a big job to sell big buildings." But he's acting like someone who's having an affair.

They'd met when Nora was searching for a small house to buy in West Seattle and Paul was her Realtor. He'd patiently shown her house after house until she'd suddenly changed her mind—realized she wasn't ready to buy an entire house, and rented a forty-foot houseboat named *Mucho Gusto* with bamboo floors on Lake Union because it was something she'd always wanted to do—live on the water, live in a floating home. Paul had warned her that houseboats required a lot of upkeep because water is corrosive and accelerates deterioration—she'd be constantly painting and varnishing. She'd moved there any-way, lived contentedly, felt more connected to the world than ever before, until marrying him a year later. They'd moved into a bungalow then, on Capitol Hill, because the constant rolling back and forth of the houseboat made him nauseated.

Paul was five years older than her, steady and ambitious. At the time she liked that—he had a life of his own and didn't need her for validation or inspiration, but now it seems, he doesn't need her for anything. Not even sex. Not that their sex life is great, or was ever great—it isn't. It wasn't. But still. Red flag waving high in the sky.

She hasn't told him about the hallucination. She's convinced herself it was a dream brought on by exhaustion, a freakish moment that's over now. There's no sense in telling him about it. She can't deny though, she is still disturbed by the girl's face, the blue eyes. Yes, the blue eyes bother her. There was something significant about them, something more than a random fleeting remnant of a nightmare.

She pushes a worn upholstered chair closer to the window, sideways so she can hear the waves and avoid the glare. Sinking into the plump cushions, she leans her head back, closes her eyes, and breathes in rhythm with the ebb and flow of the ocean. Her grandfather told her once, as they sat on the shore of Galway Bay, that on the ebb, the waves gathered up secrets and carried them away to other places, and on the flow, the secrets spilled into new places until they were heard. She'd asked him if he had ever heard any secrets but he'd just put his finger on her lips and said, *"Listen."*

In this moment, she is content.

But breathing like this, letting her guard down, is a mistake, for it is only a few minutes later when again she feels rising panic, the same agitation of air she'd felt in the classroom. She opens her eyes. There, less than ten feet away, inches above the bed, the girl's face forms out of nothingness. *Oh, my God, not again. Please, not again.* The face, obscure and veiled in blues and violets, hangs there for a few seconds and then, as quickly as before, disappears. And now here is a voice, a perfectly clear child's voice, a voice that is not in her mind, but above her, saying, *"Remember the Valentine's dress."*

Nora's heart seizes for a moment, then races and pounds loud, and before she has a chance to calm herself, to even consider what has happened, shoes bang on the stairs and Paul and Fiona burst through the door. Fiona rushes in, flushed and eager to show Nora her treasures. She holds out her yellow pail and tilts it so Nora can look inside.

"See! Aren't they pretty?"

Her daughter's voice slips around her like a lullaby, and her heart rate slows. She leans over and peers into the pail. It's hard to resist reaching in and touching the feathers and sea glass, but her hands are shaking, so she keeps them folded on her lap. "Beautiful honey, just beautiful," she says.

"I'm going to sort them into sizes and colors," Fiona says, rushing into the alcove where she will sleep.

"Honey," Nora calls to her with effort, "close the door behind you please. Mommy wants to talk with Daddy for a moment."

Fiona pauses in the doorway and looks at Nora nervously. "Mommy—is everything okay?"

"Yes, honey. Everything's fine," Nora says lightly, though of course everything is not.

"What's going on?" Paul says, once Fiona's door is closed. He sits on the edge of the bed and unties his hiking boots.

"I don't know," she whispers, drawing in a deep breath.

"What do you mean, you don't know? What's up?" He stands, pulls his T-shirt over his head, and walks over to his suitcase. He opens it and grabs a blue wrinkle-free shirt.

"I don't know. God, I . . . I . . . feel like I'm having a nervous breakdown or something."

He turns to her, buttons his shirt. "C'mon, Nora." He pulls off his jeans, pulls on his tan khakis, zips the fly. "You've just got too much on your plate, that's all. You never should have taken that department-chair job."

"Paul—"

He checks his watch. "Reservations are in fifteen minutes. Get dressed up, you'll feel better. Eat something. Christ, you're so thin! Probably half your problem." He pulls on his brown dress socks while he says all this.

She wants him to be different, to be concerned, but she knows he can't be. He's in the middle of a huge business deal and the anxiety and the pressure of it (and seductive thrill of it too, he loves this kind of stuff) is off the charts and he can't let *anything* distract him. In the beginning of their relationship, his ambitious nature—a promise of a halcyon future, more *"Clair de Lune"* than *"Ride of the Valkyries,"* his focus and drive, attracted her, but in this moment, she wants more. Kind words. An embrace. Something. But he has already walked away from her toward the mirror across the room, picked up his comb. The salty air makes his blonde hair unruly, and it's hard for him to smooth it.

"I saw something, Paul, an apparition or I hallucinated or I'm going crazy or something." She hears the instability in her voice and knows she is dangerously close to crossing a line. Still, she has told him.

He turns toward her, the comb midair. He holds her gaze longer than he has in a long time. "What the hell are you talking about?"

"I saw something. A face. A girl's face. Twice." Nora shivers and crosses her arms tightly across her chest.

"What do you mean?" He drops the comb on the dresser and looks at her, looks worried.

A lump comes up in her throat. She presses her knees together tightly. Folds her shaking hands. "In the classroom—yesterday—right after I'd dismissed the kids, I, I . . ."

He runs his hands through his hair, keeps watching her. She can't tell what he's thinking.

"I saw a girl's face. She had blue eyes. And she said—"

"A face spoke to you?" His eyes darken. Everything about his face tightens.

The window is still open and the waves shush in and out, in and out. Somewhere, the discordant squawk of a gull.

"Paul," she says, realizing she is, after all, unprepared to talk about the voice, to say what she'd heard—*Remember the Valentine's dress*— without sounding crazy and frightening him more, "would you take Fiona to dinner by yourself? I know, it's Thanksgiving, it's just that, if I rest—"

For a moment, he says nothing. Then suddenly, his face softens. "Please come with us," he says gently. He walks over to her, takes her hands and brings her to her feet. "We came here to relax, right? We're both really stressed, that's all. You probably just fell asleep for a bit, had a dream." He kisses her cheek. "Let's stop thinking of all that, okay? I'll order an amazing bottle of wine— we won't talk about work. *I* won't talk about work, I promise. We'll listen to Fiona's stories and eat and drink and come back here and sleep it off. I'll get her ready; you don't have to do a thing. Just wear what you have on." He kisses her forehead. "Okay?"

She stares at her bare feet. Thinks of Fiona. "Yes, okay," she says, her voice thin as thread.

He walks into Fiona's room and minutes later Fiona emerges, dressed in an orange sweat-shirt, jeans, and red Keds with purple laces, an outfit she'd planned especially for Thanksgiving dinner. She comes to Nora, spreads her arms wide and says, "Well, how do I look?"

"Beautiful!" Nora says. Her anxiety falls away then, and all that matters, all that she wants, is to keep that smile on Fiona's face. "You're springtime in November!"

"Thank you, Mommy," Fiona says shyly, cheeks flushing pink.

"Okay, then. Let's go! That turkey won't eat itself!" Paul says, helping a giggling Fiona with her jacket. As they leave, Nora reaches for Fiona's hand and whispers, "Happy Thanksgiving" into her wispy blonde hair.

"Happy Thanksgiving to you too, Mommy," Fiona says, clutching Nora's hand tight, and the three walk downstairs to dinner like any other family.

All eight tables in the rustic restaurant have a view of the ocean, though no one can see out because the windows are steamed up, dripping with the breath of the patrons. Everywhere, the hint of mildew and thick smell of smoke from the wood stove in the corner. Forks and knives clink on plates and voices rise and fall. Tonight there is an "All-you-can-eat Thanksgiving dinner for only $10.95!" and people are already lined up at the buffet: a young woman with a baby in a stroller, a stooped-over man holding the elbow of an elderly woman (they are wearing matching dark-green flannel shirts) who is using a walker, a young couple touching and kissing each other, everyone talking and laughing. A huge ginger cat slips between the tables, and Neil Diamond blares from the stereo. Fiona bounces with energy—a sense of camaraderie in the air. Nora is glad she came.

A waitress in her seventies with wide hips and

mostly gray hair pulled tight into a ponytail with turquoise dolphins dangling from her ears escorts them to their table.

"You're gonna want to get in line ASAP," she says. "Last year we ran out of gravy before sunset."

Paul orders *"the best Chardonnay you have,"* and they head for the line holding their big white dinner plates. There is a ten-foot long salad bar loaded with greens and toppings and also, because of the occasion, mashed potatoes, gravy, stuffing, cranberry sauce, and triangles of pumpkin pie with a plop of whipped cream on top. At the end of the salad bar a huge galvanized iron pot sits, steaming with clam chowder. A large sweaty man in a white chef's jacket stands next to the pot and slices up a gigantic roasted turkey and shouts, "Happy Thanksgiving!" every five minutes or so. Paul, Nora, and Fiona load up their plates and make their way back to the table.

Once they are seated, Paul pours the wine, flashes Nora an *I-told-you-so* smile, and they clink glasses. The cool stream of wine floats down her throat, and soon the face with the blue eyes is only a vague lingering under her ribs.

CHAPTER THREE
DECEMBER 14, 1996

Nora hadn't been able to get the face or the voice or the ache out of her head, so she'd made an appointment with her doctor. When he couldn't find anything wrong, he referred her to a neurologist who ran test after test and ruled out narcolepsy, epilepsy and Parkinson's, hemorrhages and seizures, family history, and cultural isolation.

"Cultural isolation?" Her nose wrinkled up. "But I'm a teacher."

He'd only looked at her suspiciously and asked her if she took amphetamines, marijuana, cocaine, LSD, PCP? And when she glared at him with an icy quiet, he just shrugged and said hallucinations aren't well understood and maybe she should see a psychiatrist. She'd bitten her lip. He shrugged again and said, "Emotional trauma can activate a hallucinatory region of the brain, trigger an event."

"A region? An event?" Her head began to spin, picturing wild fiestas in Spain and family reunions where everyone wears matching T-shirts—the family name emblazoned across the front.

Now, Nora sits in the psychiatrist's office,

perched on an overstuffed, green tweed couch. Dr. David Forrester sits opposite her on a chair that matches the couch. He is reviewing her medical history form, and she is impatient for him to finish reading. She doesn't like the smell of this room—lavender air freshener disguising grief, invisible clouds of uncertainty lingering and descending on those who sit here, infiltrating their heads and lips and words. A tiny clock ticks loudly on the file cabinet next to her. It faces away from her, purposefully placed, she thinks, so she won't feel the pressure of time. The doctor doesn't know it is the ticking, the ticking, the ticking in this enormous silence that creates the most pressure for her. She suddenly feels trapped and misplaced. Nearby, a ferry horn blares, and she jumps.

"Kind of loud, huh?" David says, looking up, adjusting his glasses so they are balanced evenly across his nose. She folds her hands on her lap and nods her head. He has a strong, handsome face, and a tiny silver ring glimmers from the lobe of his left ear. With his white hair and white beard he looks like a thin, hip Santa Claus.

"Well, you've got a clean health report—no medications, no allergies, no past or present disease, hormones balanced, EEG, MRI, blood work, all normal." He peers at her over his glasses for a moment before he removes them. "So let's talk. You saw a child's face, and it spoke to you."

His tone is gentle, nonjudgmental, which of course it would be—psychiatrists are trained for this sort of thing. She'd hoped though, for a bit of surprise from him, some reaction to suggest he knew she was not the type who hears voices.

She flushes a bit and nods. "Yes, a face, but no body."

He folds over page one and begins reading page two. Without looking up, he says, "And your sleep is worsening; you have nightmares, and you feel unable to cope with everyday things." He looks at her for confirmation. She nods again.

"Can you tell me more about feeling unable to cope?"

"Well—" she says quietly, "I . . . just feel so tense all the time. And the smallest thing, things that don't seem to bother anyone else, make me feel like I want to break something, and lately it seems worse, and I get these strange headaches that no one seems to be able to explain, and—" she is suddenly aware of her quick acceleration of thoughts and stops abruptly. She does not want to fail at appearing normal.

"Do you remember when the first *strange* headache began?"

She closes her eyes. She remembers when it started—three weeks ago at Fiona's birthday party.

"Six more days until my birthday!" Fiona announced at breakfast a week before her birthday, holding up six fingers. And then every breakfast after that: "Five more days!" "Four more days!" "Three more days!" "Two more days!" "One more day!" Until finally, she shouted from the top of the stairs, "Today's the day! Today I'm six years old!"

And what a beautiful day they had. Nora took Fiona and five of her friends (three girls and two boys because Fiona wanted exactly six kids) on the Metro bus to Golden Gardens, their favorite waterfront park because it has the most sand. Paul (he worked Saturdays) planned to meet them for lunch.

Nora sat at a weathered picnic table, the salty air filling her lungs, quickening her senses, and watched the children race up and down the beach in their parkas and little rubber boots. They picked up shells, jumped over tide pools, and dodged waves as they broke upon the beach, their boot prints trailing behind, tiny imprints vanishing in a flash with the next foamy wave.

Her little girl running closest to the waves, fiercely innocent, daring the waves to catch her, and then running away fast, laughing and shouting, "You can't get me! You can't get me!"

When had this happened? When had the milky-breathed infant who sucked hungrily at her breast grown up enough to dare the ocean? Where was the toddler with the chubby legs who waddled about the house, feeding Oreos to her

25

stuffed animals and holding books upside down, pretending to read?

It was then, in this delicious, bittersweet musing, that the headache began to pound.

"Nora? Nora, did you hear me? Do you remember when the headaches started?"

"It was Fiona's—my daughter's—birthday party. Three weeks ago. Her sixth birthday." Her mouth is dry, and it's hard to swallow.

"Did you enjoy the party?"

"Yes. Yes, it was wonderful." Despite her headache, the day had been perfect. Paul had arrived in time for lunch, and Fiona was thrilled at the sight of him. She'd laughed hysterically with her friends as he sang a solo of "Happy Birthday" in a low, rumbling voice and gave her six big kisses, three on each cheek. In that moment, Nora's heart had brimmed. Sitting at a picnic table, in this little circle of love with her husband and six children, all with purple lips from the cupcakes—this is how it was supposed to be.

"Six years old. A sweet age," David says.

Nora's eyes well up, and she wants to be home. She wants to decorate the house for Christmas. It's Saturday morning and she should be home making hot chocolate for Fiona instead of here in this stale room pushing the edges of her mind to god knows where.

"This has to be hard, feeling so tired while trying to be a good mother and teacher at the same time," he says.

His kindness unnerves her. She presses her back deeper into the couch, presses her knees together with her folded hands between her thighs.

"Nora, before this—before the headaches, nightmares, and hallucinations—how did you feel?"

She shrugs. "Fine, I guess." And she does think that. Mostly. But then, there's that small, weighted part of her that feels like she's lying, the part that fires an adrenaline rush through her every time someone asks how she is.

"Were you happy?"

She is caught off guard, flustered. The question is so personal. She flushes more deeply, stares at her folded hands.

He looks at the page and up again. "And you rate your marriage a three out of ten?"

"Yes," she says, her face burning now. "It's just that . . . I don't know." She stops speaking. It all feels too intimate to tell a stranger, and besides, she's here to talk about the face.

David folds his hands on her pile of forms. "Hmmm," he says finally. "So you have a lot of stress."

She pulls a pillow onto her lap, a beige canvas one with a huge bird on it—a black raven made from felt stitched on with red thread. She likes ravens, she relates to their preference for privacy.

"Stress can trigger hallucinations."

"And make you crazy?" She traces the raven with her finger.

"I know you're frightened, but using words like that doesn't help, only scares you. We'll need to have many conversations before I can even make a diagnosis—"

She closes her eyes. Continues to trace the raven. Wants to throw it in the air and see if it will fly. "Christ," she says.

"Listen, I'm sure you've heard about experiments on sleep deprivation, how it significantly decreases normal functioning—can cause depression, anxiety, reduce cognitive ability . . ."

She opens her eyes and stops tracing the raven. She stares at him.

"A lack of sleep can cause personality distortions. Even just forty-eight hours can do that. After three days people have been known to hallucinate."

"What are the chances I'm not crazy?" She hears herself asking this question and can hardly bear that at this point in her life, this is where she is, on this couch, with this pillow, asking this question.

"Again, please stop using that word. I'll be a broken record if I need to be."

She crosses and recrosses her legs. She doesn't want to offend him. "Sorry," she says.

He leans forward, fixes his eyes on hers. "I

become concerned when a person loses the ability to interpret hallucinations or voices as a problem. *You* seem very clear that something is wrong. Whether it's chemical or emotional is for us to find out. And let me be clear with you. There are many in the medical field who are quick to label something like this a disorder, who are quick to prescribe medication, and well, I believe it's worth looking at other things first—factors outside of our immediate awareness—thoughts, feelings, experiences that influence us, many of which we are not conscious of. Obviously, I'm here to help you explore those factors in a safe environment. I'm not saying I won't prescribe medication—I *will* if I feel it's necessary—but there's a lot more to be done before we make that decision."

She gazes at the closed aluminum blinds on the only window as if they are open. Bits of light poke through the holes where the strings attach to the slats. She wants to trust him.

He leans forward. "More people than you might think, so-called 'normal' people"—he makes quotation marks with his fingers—"report such visions."

This is not easy to believe. She doesn't know anyone who's had hallucinations and *not* been on drugs, *not* been psychotic. What if she believes him when in reality she needs medication? What if she walks out the door feeling normal only to have a hallucination in her classroom tomorrow?

"Nora, what's going on right now?" He takes off his glasses and cleans them on his shirt. "What are you feeling?"

She can't get a grip on this question. Her mind is clouded, tangled, and worn out. Worn out with visions and the thinking about visions and what's normal and what isn't, and the new things: this man, this office, these ideas, this ticking clock, this pillow, this couch.

He looks at the clock.

"We have twenty more minutes," he says, settling back in his chair. "May I ask you a few questions about the face?"

She nods.

"Were your eyes open when you saw her?"

"Yes, the first time I saw her, I'm pretty sure my eyes were open," she says quietly. "And yes, the second time my eyes were open. I was sitting in a chair looking out the window, resting." She sounds apologetic, as if she shouldn't have been sitting in a chair, resting.

"Did you recognize her? Could it have been Fiona?"

"No. No, it wasn't Fiona. Fiona's eyes are blue, but they're a gray blue. And they weren't my eyes either. These eyes were the bluest blue, deep sea blue. Not like any eyes I've ever seen. The rest of the image was blurry. Just shapes really. Like seeing a face through water." Her stomach is beginning to hurt.

"But you know it was a child's face."

"Yes."

"What did she say?"

"Something like, 'Remember the Valentine's dress.'"

"Does that mean anything to you?"

"I don't know. My grandmother sent me a dress once, for Valentine's Day. I think I was maybe five or six years old."

"Can you describe it?"

"Well, I'd never seen anything like it before. It was so beautiful. Red. And it had a white collar with two embroidered roses and—" Nora pauses, feeling her description sounds childish.

"Were you close to your grandmother?"

"No, not really. I was closest to my grandfather. I lived with them in Ireland after my mother died," she says quietly. "James, my little brother, and I lived with them. My mother was born there and after she died, my father left us with her parents and then . . . he never came back." After a moment, she adds, "I have no idea where he is."

"I see." He flips through the forms. "So your mother was Irish, and your father—"

"American. German American. Well, his parents were German."

"Did you ever hear from him again?"

"He wrote us a couple of times, and we wrote him, but after awhile, the letters were returned." She thinks now, with a slight ache, of all those letters she'd written. *Dear Daddy, where are you? When are you coming back for us?*

"And when did your mother die? I don't see anything about either of your parents here."

She wonders where she might have written about her parents. There had been a section called "Other Pertinent Information," but it hadn't occurred to her to write about her parents. She doesn't think of herself as having parents. "I was eleven and James was five," she says.

"You were both very young."

"There was an accident," Nora says stiffly.

"An accident?"

She hasn't thought about the accident in a long time. She used to obsess about it, running it over and over in her mind. And then one day (she'd just turned thirteen), she'd stood with her grandfather at the end of the jetty, both of them gazing across the Irish Sea, and he had turned to her, had taken her hands into his, looked her hard in the eyes. "Nora, it wasn't your fault. You were a child. A precious child. It wasn't your fault." She remembered his expression, his blue eyes as serious as the sea, and how gusts of wind had carried the scent of hawthorn blossoms to them and how she'd thrown herself against him and sobbed into his chest. And how, after that moment, as they walked home along the shore, the world had suddenly tilted into the light— the water glistening with silver threads, dazzling filaments blowing into the sky.

CHAPTER FOUR
1969

Nora pounds the keys on the old piano in the basement, pounds it out, *Don't make it bad,* pounds it out, the bruises still raw and red on her face, pounds it out, *Don't let her under your skin,* drowns it out. Her mother still screaming from the top of the stairs, *"Stop that goddamn noise,"* her mother's words mud thick, suffocating in gin. Nora, in her plaid school uniform and saddle shoes, doesn't stop, doesn't stop beating the song into herself, absorbing the flats and sharps, *Let it out and let it in.*

But now, a shriek from the top of the stairs, and now, a great thud, and Nora stops beating the keys and twists around and sees the body of her mother, falling. The arms and legs, hips and hands, neck and mouth of her mother crashing down the basement stairs, the glass shattering. And now, a green olive—the green olive alive, moving fast and wild, announcing the falling body, bouncing and coming to a halt next to the black part of Nora's left shoe.

And then, a final sudden thud.

For a long while, Nora waits stock-still in the dead silence, staring at the motionless body, the belly and breasts flattened, the head turned unnaturally to the side, tangled auburn hair obscuring the eyes, nothing moving at all. Finally, Nora stands up and steps over the green olive and walks to the phone and dials "0." She gasps to the operator, "My mother, it's my mother."

And the operator says, warm as milk, "Someone will be there honey, someone will be there soon."

Blood pools from under her mother's head, pools on the black-and-white checked linoleum, rivulets of red traveling toward Nora and she is frozen there, holding the phone, the operator still saying things in her ear.

Now there are medics and emergency shouts, and a man's voice says, "No pulse!" and someone steps on the green olive and flattens it.

And now, here is Nora standing tight and hunched, in the hush of church, staring with bare eyes into the casket, holding her father's big hand, the red heat of her guilt eclipsing her bruises, now gone violet on her cheeks.

And when her father drops her hand to hold his own weeping face, Nora reaches tentatively into the casket and touches the hands of her mother. The hands are cold and she is taken aback for a moment. But now, she begins to stroke the hands, trace the bones and curves with her index finger, trace the lines of the knuckles, the ashen hands inert, dead without the rage, and Nora is startled, startled to feel the skin is so delicate, fragile as Bible paper.

CHAPTER FIVE
DECEMBER 20, 1996

Nora stares at the fingers of her right hand as they twist the wedding ring around the finger on her left hand. Lately, she's been thinking of not wearing the ring at all.

"Can you tell me more about your mother?" David asks. It's been a week since her last visit, a week since she'd told him about her mother's fall.

"That's a pretty general question, don't you think?" She immediately regrets her tone, unsure of her resistance to this line of questioning; he's been so kind to her. "I'm sorry," she says.

"No worries. Let me rephrase."

She nods, stops twisting the ring, and reaches for the raven pillow. Sets it on her lap. Folds her hands together on top.

"What else might be important for me to know about your mother?"

One of Fiona's favorite books, *The Important Book*, comes to her mind. *The important thing about a spoon is you eat with it. It's like a little shovel. The important thing about a shoe is you put your foot in it. You walk with it.*

"Nora?"

"I don't know." She can feel herself struggling

for something more to say about her mother. She hadn't felt a thing when telling of the accident. She'd long ago buried any feelings for her mother. She needs to talk about the face and the voice, but she is unable to say so and doesn't know why.

"Nora?"

She refolds her hands. "I guess it's important that she was fifteen when she emigrated to America. And seventeen when she married my father."

He raises his eyebrows. "Pretty young to leave home—to come so far."

Nora thinks of a Polaroid she keeps in the bottom drawer of her desk. She hasn't looked at it for years, hasn't felt the need. Her father had given it to her after the funeral. "Your mother used to be happy," he'd said and dropped the picture on her desk. "Damned alcohol."

In the picture her mother and father are young and look like they don't need anything else in the world but each other. They're already married (a diamond sparkles from her mother's finger) and are living in Chicago. They are sitting at a round wooden table in a dark bar. Her mother wears a sleeveless, low-cut red dress, her wavy auburn hair loose, falling onto her exposed cleavage. She is laughing, holding out a martini to the camera as if toasting it, her bright white teeth flashing against red lipstick, her other arm around Nora's father. She looks like a movie star, like Maureen O'Hara. Nora's father holds a cigarette, wears a large gold watch, and is smiling at her mother, looks as if he might kiss her.

"Nora? Did you hear me? That's pretty far for such a young woman to travel."

She looks away from him. Stares at the closed blinds. "My grandfather said that of all his eight children, she was the wildest—the one born for adventure. The bravest one." And now these words, *"The bravest one,"* breathe out a lost memory.

Nora is fourteen. Lying in bed. Her aunts and her grandmother talking in the kitchen. The aunts visit on Sundays. They sit around the large kitchen table with their mother, drinking whiskey in their black tea and eating pie and having interesting conversations about recipes, neighbors, love, and death. Nora hears her mother's name, Maeve. She creeps down the hall and listens at the doorway.

"I miss Maeve more than anything," Claire whispers. Claire is the younger of the two aunts. She is tall and beautiful with long black hair. She lives down the road with her husband and three little boys.

"Ach," her grandmother says, sadness filling her voice. "It was wildness killed that one."

"Mam! It wasn't her wildness killed her, and ye know it!" Claire cries.

Nora stands there in the hall in her flannel pajamas and wool socks. She stands very still.

"Hush!" her grandmother says. "She was fifteen. What would ye have had us do? Would ye rather all of us be called out in contempt every Sunday in church? Would ye have had those damned nuns pounding on our door, day after day demanding we put her in those evil homes or burn in hell? They'd have had her washing laundry until her fingers were raw." And now her grandmother's voice is deathly flat. "Sending her to America was the best we could do. She's lucky my sister took her in, aye, and was willing to take her to that doctor."

"And what of Seamus?" her aunt Caroline says angrily. Caroline is the oldest sister, an unmarried woman who runs a bakery in town. "Sure he walks around town like he owns the place, no one even knowing it is him who was the father and poor Maeve sent off full of shame for a secret abortion and now . . . now she's—" Caroline is crying now. "Sure 'n' I hope I never have a girl in this damned country."

Nora stands, openly now, in the doorway. Tears stream down her face. "My mother had an abortion?"

"Jesus, Mary, and Joseph," her grandmother says, reaching her arms out to Nora then, but it is Claire Nora runs to, pressing herself into her aunt's breasts. "Jesus, Mary, and Joseph," her grandmother says again and again. And now, Caroline's arms around her too. The three of them weeping into the silences of loss, guilt, and shame.

Later, in bed, Nora cried hard again, thinking of her mother, only a year older than herself, exposed on the doctor's table, legs spread wide, the doctor sucking the baby out with a machine. "Mommy," she'd cried.

"Nora," David says. "Are you okay? Would you like some water?"

Nora stands and walks over to the blinds. Pulls the cord so they open slightly. Outside, a female parking attendant with white gloves slashes a yellow line of chalk across a car tire. She moves from car to car, in her navy uniform with its orange vest, gray hair poking out from her hat. She bends and rises, making her mark over and over again.

Nora adjusts the blinds until only a bit of light comes through. "My mother was so pretty," she says into the slats. "Beautiful. Especially when my father came home at night. She wore lipstick. A light shade of pink. Sometimes she'd put it on my lips, and we'd dress up in her cocktail dresses and waltz around the house to the Kingston Trio." She turns toward David. "She loved to sing 'Tom Dooley.' She'd pick up a hairbrush and pretend she was Dave Guard—you know, one of the Kingston Trio? Her voice was amazing."

"What else do you remember?"

Nora sits on the windowsill. "Her skin was soft. She told me once how her mother sometimes warmed up milk in a huge pot on the stove, to soften her face and her sisters' faces—that's how Irish women kept themselves beautiful. And before I went to bed sometimes, she'd dab my face with Pond's Cold Cream and tell me I had beautiful skin, too."

"Lovely."

"But then—"

"What?"

"I don't know. She stopped being pretty. I don't remember exactly when. I only remember that her lips tightened into a hard line, and she stopped wearing lipstick. And she had a shot or two of gin every day around three." Nora hears her speech become more agitated, but she keeps going. "Sometimes she would sit at the kitchen table with her head in her hands and cry. I felt sorry for her, but she was just so . . ."

"So *what,* Nora?"

"Just so fucking—" *Did I just say "fucking" out loud?* She can feel a headache beginning and presses her fingers into her temples.

"So fucking . . . ?" David repeats her words as calmly as if she had said, "*So very.*"

God, it must be easy to become a therapist, she thinks. *You basically take the last word the client says and repeat it back to them in the form of*

40

a question. She is tempted to tell him her mind feels too blurry, that his questions and important books, abortions and shots of gin are all colliding in her head, making it hard to concentrate.

"Nora, is there something else?"

She walks back to the couch and sits down. Crosses her right leg over the left. The foot of the right leg moves back and forth, back and forth. She watches it for a moment then stops it. The shoe on the foot is untied. She reaches over to tie it, but her fingers are trembling. She uncrosses her legs and presses her knees together.

"Is there something else you'd like to say, Nora?"

Silence.

She knows what she *should* say; she should tell David that sometimes her mother would shriek at her and how if she tried to run her mother would grab her, throw her down, bring her hand hard across her cheek, how the force of the slap sent her reeling against walls and furniture, how sharp and shocking those things felt against her body. She should have told him how her mother pulled her hair out, how she had wanted her mother to die.

Instead she says, "She was sick. She was sad." Nora reaches for the raven pillow, places it on her lap, and clenches her hands together on top of the bird's beak. "An alcoholic."

"Nora," he says in an overtly gentle tone, "Did she hurt you?"

She focuses on the oak shelves overflowing with books: *Cognitive Behavioral Therapy*, *Feeling Good: The New Mood Therapy*, *Mental Health or Mental Illness?*, *Stations of the Mind*, *The Diagnostic and Statistical Manual of Mental Disorders*, *Foundations of Psychology*, *In a Different Voice*, *Society's Betrayal of the Child*—

"Being an alcoholic doesn't mean you have the right to hurt your children," he says.

"I don't see any Freud, any Jung," she says, still staring at the books. "Kind of weird."

"I have a complicated relationship with them," he says. "I just think overgeneralizing about what's masculine and what's feminine is slippery, you know? The perpetuation of gender myths— but Nora, did you hear what I said? Your mother didn't have the right to hurt you."

"I get why you might not have Freud; the penis-projection theory pisses me off, but I mean, would you even be here without his whole face-to-face talk-therapy thing? It just seems like you'd have at least one book—"

"Nora, is this really what you want to talk about?"

"You don't think it's important I know what you believe when it comes to the psyche? Seriously. Isn't it a good thing we're aware of archetypal images and confront our feminine and masculine selves? Correct the fucking patriarchal consciousness? And what about how he dared to face the unconscious self? Jesus. How can you *as a therapist* not have a book on Jung?"

"Like I said, I have a complicated relationship with him. I just don't happen to think consciousness has a gender. And it seems a tad misogynistic to me that when he wrote about feminine qualities they were always tied to inferiority."

She had forgotten this and wonders why, because it is something she should have remembered. Maybe it's because of all the stress of remembering things in here—makes it hard to think clearly. Whatever—she is glad they're talking about Jung instead of her mother.

"I had a high school science teacher who praised me once for thinking like a guy, and it really pissed me off," she says.

He leans down to get his Stanley thermos. Unscrews the attached cup and puts it between his knees while he unscrews the black cover on top of the thermos. He pours coffee into the cup, screws the cover back on, and sets the thermos under his chair. He sips the coffee and says, "I see a lot of people in my practice, and I'm hard-pressed to come up with generalizations based on gender. Women who are assertive and driven should not be called masculine, and men who display passivity or emotion should not automatically have their masculinity questioned. Totally damages self-esteem." He takes another sip of coffee. "And there's plenty of new research to support that what is thought of as masculine or feminine is actually culturally determined." He leans back into his chair.

She thinks then of how much her father hated when James cried. How much he hated when James played dolls with her. How, when James wanted to be a pink tulip for Halloween, her father said, *"No son of mine is going to be a goddamn pansy."*

"Nora, could we get back to your mother before the time is up? You heard me say your mother had no right to hit you, right?"

She looks at the clock and sees there's ten minutes left in the session. Ten minutes is a very long time, especially now that he's gone back to talking about her mother. "Yes. I heard you and I know that," she says and tosses the raven pillow off her lap. She stands and plucks her coat from the coat rack.

"Nora, what's going on for you right now?" He sits on the edge of his chair with his hands wrapped around his cup.

She faces him, struggling to put her coat on. "What about this don't you understand? I SAW A FACE. I HEARD A VOICE." Her voice is louder than she wants it to be, which alarms her. The tension between past and present makes her want to grab the raven pillow and shove it down his throat.

44

"We're just connecting the dots," he says.

She buttons her coat. Stares at the black buttons. Closes her eyes. *Dots.* In her mind, the dots crowd together and she is a dot and there are so many dots crowding her, too many dots and the dot of her has disappeared in the oppressive mud of dots that stinks like shit and there's no place to breathe and the mud has already swallowed her. *This is why she probably needs medication.*

"Sit down, Nora," he says. "Please. Sit down."

She opens her eyes and stares at him until her eyes are focused again. She can see by the expression on his face, half alarmed and half sympathetic, he has doubts. "I need to go home," she says, more to herself than to him, and flies out the door. Running home she tells herself things: *You are fine* and *This too will pass,* and by the time she arrives home she almost believes it.

"Mommy's home!" Fiona yells from the front door. She's wearing her red wool jacket and red rubber boots. Her face scrunched pink with worry and anger, her arms folded. "Mommy! Did you forget about the Christmas tree?"

Paul stands in the doorway, tense and upset, glaring at her as if she were a problem child.

"You're late," he says. She doesn't know what time it is, but she can't be more than ten or fifteen minutes late.

"We've been waiting for over an hour," he says.

"A whole hour!" Fiona says.

"Geez, I'm sorry," Nora says, shocked to find out about the time. She'd taken the scenic route, walked along the waterfront to calm herself. She'd needed the ocean smell, the rush of salty wind on her face, but it couldn't have taken an hour. Unsure of what to say or do, she bends down to put Fiona's hood up and tie it snugly.

"Stop, Mommy! That's too tight!" Fiona protests, pulls Nora's hands off the hood strings, gives her mother a frightened glance.

"It's not that cold," Paul says, tightly. "She doesn't need a hood."

The clouds are heavy with snow, and the tips of Nora's fingers sting, but she holds her tongue. She stands and drops her hands to her sides, feeling stupid and alien, as if she doesn't live in this house, as if this isn't her daughter or her husband. Fiona bites her lip, says, "You're the worst mom ever."

Nora's heart stalls. Her cheeks redden. She resists the urge to crumple. She takes a deep breath and stares at Fiona, stares at her until she knows what to say next. Fiona glares back, fists clenched, says, "The worst," but then her eyes well up with tears.

"Oh, sweetheart," Nora says, filled with tenderness for her daughter. She bends down, takes Fiona's mittened hands in hers, kisses her wet cheeks, her long eyelashes. "Honey, I am really sorry I'm late. Really sorry." Nora kisses her little cold nose, the tiny bone of it, says, "Sometimes mommies mess up, make mistakes. But listen! We've got hours until it's dark! Let's go get that tree! Let's get a huge one!"

Fiona sniffles. Looks at Nora as if gauging the truth of her mother's words.

Nora kisses her nose again. "Everything's okay, bug," Nora says. "Please don't worry."

"Can we get a tree that touches the ceiling?" Fiona whimpers, still a bit uncertain.

"We'll get the perfect one!" Paul says, suddenly forgiving, suddenly kind, making Fiona's worry fade, making her smile. "We'll get one so tall, we'll need a ladder to put the star on top!"

"This will be fun," Nora says, "I'll just run quick to the bathroom and be right back."

She shuts the bathroom door, sits on the edge of the tub and puts her face in her hands. Blood pulses against her temples. Her hands form into fists. She is angry. Angry at herself for being late. She bangs her fists against her head. Angry at David for making her talk about her mother. Bang, bang, bang.

In her mind she is seven, hiding in the bathroom with James, her hands pressed over his ears, trying to block out the voices of their parents fighting and slamming doors, slamming each other. Bang, bang, bang.

Paul revs the car engine outside the window. She needs to compose herself. "You are not your mother," she whispers. "You are not your mother. And you will go out in the car with your family and chop down the tree." She unclenches her fists slowly. "You will chop down the Christmas tree." She pushes herself up from the tub, leaves the bathroom, walks outside, and gets in the car.

Fiona sings from the back seat: "Silent night, foamily night, all is calm, all is bright, 'round John Virgin, another child."

Paul is staring straight ahead, his eyes fixated on the taxi parked in front of them. The taxi driver is holding the cab door open for a lovely young woman, maybe thirty, who looks as though she is dressed for the opera. She glances their way and for a moment it seems she might wave, but then she quickly steps inside the cab. Nora wonders if they've met before, asks Paul if he knows her. "No idea," he says nonchalantly.

Nora smiles at Fiona then and begins to sing along with her, determined her daughter will feel what children ought to feel at this time of year. And for the second time that day, she thinks she might cry—something she hasn't done for a long time—a sensation that startles her. *Children ought not sing Christmas carols alone.*

CHAPTER SIX
DECEMBER 21, 1996

"I'm seeing a psychiatrist," Nora says to John, her breath pulsing little clouds into the cold air, her heart racing with the worry of how much to expose. They're strolling side by side around the school grounds, shoes crunching on dirty crusted snow over gravel, making their presence known to the smokers and potheads, not because they're particularly concerned (they're not, they both smoked plenty in high school), but because the parents need reassurance their kids are well looked after.

Nora and John sign up for the early morning patrol year after year because no one else wants to do it, and it's given them time to become friends, to get to know each other beyond their professional lives. He knows how much she loves being a mother, how she'd do anything for Fiona, that she'd never known such love was possible, how the surge and pulse of it continually startles her and makes her want to be a better person. He knows how she practically stops breathing when she talks about a student who's written words that cut to the core, who's found a true way to express what they feel. He knows she loves to write poetry and will stay up late into the night until she finds just the right word, the accurate shape to describe something she'd seen that day, and that she'd like to climb through the underground cities of Cappadocia just to feel the ancient dirt under her nails.

Nora knows things about him too: That he was adopted by a Seattle couple (a gynecologist and a fourth-grade teacher) when he was a baby and that his birth parents were teenaged Cherokee kids and that sometimes he wonders where he'd be if he'd been born after the Indian Child Welfare Act. He's shy, never married. He doesn't like to cook and eats takeout while watching PBS documentaries or reading Faulkner. Sometimes he goes to powwows in Spokane or Yakima, but mostly he feels he's not really welcome, that he's just tolerated, treated like a spectator, a blunt instrument, a fraud, and he comes home depressed and unable to sleep for weeks because sounds of drumming, constant drumming, keep his eyes open.

"A psychiatrist?" he says, but now there is something in his voice that doesn't sound right. "Really? But you're one of the strongest people I know."

Nora wraps her arms around herself, her fingers still cold through her gloves. "I've been having nightmares, and . . ." But she can't do it. She can't tell him about the face, about the voice whispering "Remember the Valentine's dress."

She looks away. A few boys walk by, huddled and hunched under their backpacks, eyes to the ground. The bell rings.

"Nora, can we talk more about this after school?"

"I have to pick up Fiona . . ."

"Listen, vacation starts tomorrow, and if you want to take a few days off after that, if you need more time—"

"I'll be fine," she says and walks away, heart in her throat.

CHAPTER SEVEN
DECEMBER 22, 1996

The next day, Nora dismisses thoughts of the hallucinations and prepares for Christmas, even though her relationship with God is rocky. She's never understood the arbitrary nature of God, the logic behind *"some are blessed and some are damned,"* hates when people exclaim, *"I'm so blessed!"* every time they get a parking spot or survive cancer, as if people who can't find a parking spot or die from cancer aren't blessed and should work harder to earn God's favor and protection. She'd stopped capitalizing "god" and attending Mass in secondary school when she learned about the Holocaust, saw photos of naked bodies piled high, knees and arms bent, shaved heads with their eyes open but not focused.

And it wasn't only a matter of her not believing in God. She'd felt for a long time God didn't believe in her either. She doesn't remember when exactly this vague realization came to her, but she knows she was five or six when Sister Catherine emphatically told the entire class, *"God loves you; there is nothing you can do to make God stop loving you,"* and Nora had squirmed in her chair and felt with an absolute certainty this was not true for her. But maybe the doubt had come later, maybe it was when her mother had fallen down the stairs and died. Nora remembers how questions—*Why would God love me anyway? Why should God love me?*—had circled like sharks in her brain.

She remembers when she'd told her grandfather she no longer believed in a monotheistic God, could no longer attend Mass. A Sunday morning in 1975. She'd just turned fourteen. He was piling turf onto the fire, and the smoky dirt scent of it, the ancient plant and animal of it, permeated the room.

"Your grandmother already left for Mass," he'd said into the red sparks. "Ye best run fast to catch up with her."

She stood there in her wool sweater and jeans, her feet bare on the slate floor. "I'm not going to Mass anymore," she'd said.

He prodded the turf more than necessary. He prodded so long she said, "Grandfather?" her heart loud against its bony cage.

He'd stood then and faced her, his blue eyes intent upon hers for several moments.

"Well now, you're old enough to decide then, I suppose," he'd said and sat down in his chair, picked up the *Irish Times*, and began to read.

Her grandmother only commented about her decision once. Nora lay reading Sylvia Plath in bed that evening, and her grandmother came quiet into the room. She stood at the end of the bed, her reddened, rough hands wrapped tight around the foot rail. "You've broken me heart," she said, and when Nora opened her mouth, had intended to argue, to explain, her grandmother crossed herself and said, "We'll say nothing more about it," and left the room.

Ever since, Nora had enjoyed living her own life, had enjoyed setting her own terms and conditions, but when she'd become pregnant with Fiona and felt a heart pulse within her, the tiny bones fluttering against the soft inside of her belly, lighting the closed spaces, she'd allowed "god" to become synonymous with love. Simple as that.

But she wants Fiona to believe in magic, wants to ease the tension in the household, so she wraps presents and signs them, *"Love, Santa,"* and winds strings of white lights through the limbs of the spruce tree in the living room. Fiona helps her, sings carols and throws bunches of silver icicles on the branches, stepping back every few moments to clap her hands and exclaim, "Oh Mommy, it's magic!" Nora watches her and wants to freeze the moment, wants to remember every enchanting detail.

Paul brings them a small gift each night: one night, a pair of hand-knit orange mittens for Fiona, a lavender candle for Nora. "For the twelve days of Christmas," he says as he hands them each a wrapped box, always tied with a pretty ribbon, each time kissing Fiona on the cheek and Nora quickly on the lips.

She tries not to think about who else he is kissing. She's more convinced now than ever that he's having an affair, though she really doesn't have any good evidence, only that he's been working later and later each night, and by the time she wakes up in the morning, he's gone. She could ask him about it, straight out, the way he likes things, direct—she could say, *"Are you having an affair?"* but she fears that if anything else should go wrong right now, that if he answered her, *"Yes, Nora, I love someone else,"* she might lose her mind once and for all, and so she keeps silent until she feels strong enough for the truth.

"Oh, Daddy!" Fiona says one night when he gives her a book called *The Mitten.* The three of them sit around the sparkling Christmas tree to read it even though it's way past her bedtime. Paul had come home late, and Nora had allowed Fiona to wait up for him.

"It's about a little boy in Ukraine," Paul says, as Fiona climbs onto his lap with the book. "Ukraine is close to where my grandparents lived."

"In Poland!" Fiona says, proud to have remembered.

It surprises Nora that Paul is talking about his family. He rarely does. Fiona knows his grandparents immigrated to America—New York, had changed their name from Bronowski to Brown. She knows his father was in the Korean War, same as Nora's father, and that his father was a pilot—that his plane was shot down and he was a hero. But Paul hasn't told her about his mother. They'd both agreed that Fiona was too young to know what really happened—that at nineteen, he'd found his mother in the closet, hanging by his father's best Sunday tie. That, as her only child, Paul had tried for a decade to draw her out of sadness, quit school to make money for them, but nothing had worked. They remained in poverty, and it was only much later he'd realized she'd been manic-depressive. Sometimes, to Nora, it seems like he still believes that if he makes enough money, she'll come back to him.

"I'm sad your mommy and daddy died," Fiona says, hugging him.

"Me too," he says. "Me too."

He looks so sad that for a second Nora thought he might cry, but then he says, "Let's read the story, okay?" And he reads it to her twice, until she is asleep in his arms, and he carries her upstairs to bed. When he returns, he says, "She's ready for her goodnight kiss."

"Okay." Nora is in the living room trying to write a Kafkaesque poem about a woman who woke up with a book for an arm and was overcome by the feeling that other parts of her body might grow into books and she might be reduced to paper and words and become unrecognizable to herself and to others.

"I've got some work to catch up on; don't wait up, okay?" he says.

His words an arrow between her eyes. "There are pork chops in the oven," she says. "And some cheesy broccoli." She is disappointed he isn't going to sit by the tree with her.

"I grabbed a tuna sandwich from the deli," he says. "But again, thanks." He's lying about the sandwich, and she can see it in his eyes. Her chest begins a slow ache.

"The Redmond deal's almost cinched," he says then, as if reading her mind and wanting to change the subject so they don't have a fight that goes on and on. "It's almost in the bag, Nora. I'll get a promotion. More money."

"Do we need more money?"

"That's not the point. Why can't you say, 'Good luck!' or, 'I know you can do it!' "

"Well, I know you can do it," she says. "Good luck." But he has already walked away and doesn't hear her sarcasm. This is what happens when two people begin to separate.

CHAPTER EIGHT
DECEMBER 24, 1996

Her brother, James, is coming from Chicago for Christmas and bringing his new partner, Stephen, who is a doctor. "A pediatrician with a talent for intuitive assessment and a reputation for not over-prescribing medications," James told her months ago during their Sunday phone call. "I can't wait for you to meet him!"

Nora buys fragrant white roses and places them in modern rectangular glass vases on each nightstand in the guest room where James and Stephen will sleep. While she arranges things, she hears in her head, unexpectedly, her father singing "The Christmas Rose," like he did when she was small, as he tucked her into bed. *The flower so small, whose sweet fragrance fills the air, dispels with glorious splendor the darkness everywhere.* Remembering this, she feels a tightening in her stomach. Perhaps she misses her father after all, that maybe even after all this time, there's a bit of love left, a weed pushing through a sidewalk crack. But now her hand is flying, and now the vase of flowers is on the floor, rose petals pierced with splinters of glass, and water, a mess at her feet.

The doorbell rings and Fiona runs to open it.

She is wearing her bluebird pajamas and the plastic rhinestone tiara Paul had given her last year for her birthday.

"Uncle James," she squeals.

"Hey, pipsqueak!" James says, laughing as he sets his suitcase down, sweeping her up into his arms. Stephen stands by his side, grinning. He is tall and slender and appears slightly older than James, who is now thirty-three. His fine brown hair falls across his forehead, and his face is clean-shaven, a sharp contrast to James' unruly red curls and scruff of beard that's at least a week old.

"Fiona, this is Stephen."

"Hi, Fiona," Stephen says, his voice soft, his green eyes filled with warmth.

"Come on in and see our tree!" Fiona says, squirming down, taking each of their hands and pulling them toward the living room, gusts of winter air blowing in behind them.

"Wait, wait, love," James says, closing the door behind him. "I need to hug my big sister!" James hugs Nora then, lifting her off the ground. "Merry Christmas Eve, Sis! Sorry we missed dinner."

"It's so good to see you. I can't believe it's been a year," Nora says once he's set her back down.

Stephen embraces her too, kissing her on both cheeks. She likes him already.

"James, Stephen," Paul says, offering a strained smile and a handshake to each of them. Nora hears the tightness in his voice, a constriction that finds its way to her, making her nervous. This is the first time James has brought a boyfriend to their home overnight, and Paul isn't happy about it. He still thinks being gay is a choice, a bad one.

"It's not a choice; it's biological," she'd argued each time, his statements making her furious. She'd even thrown a plate at him once, but he'd ducked, and it had shattered against the wall.

"C'mon," Fiona calls from the living room. "Look, Uncle James!" she says pointing to a plaster of paris decoration near the top of the tree. James plucks it off, obviously delighted.

"What's this?" Stephen says, laughing, taking it from the palm of James' hand and holding it up to eye-level.

"It's Uncle James' handprint from kindergarten," Fiona giggles, her face flushed.

"A born artist," Stephen says, putting his arm around James and placing the decoration back on the tree as if it is the most precious thing. The two sink into the couch with Fiona giggling on top of them while Paul lights the fire. Nora enters the room carrying a wooden tray with bottles of pinot noir and sparkling cider, glasses, and a plate of sugar cookies shaped like stars. She sets the tray on the coffee table and pours cider into a glass for Fiona.

"Mommy and me made the cookies!" Fiona exclaims, scrambling off Stephen's lap and grabbing a cookie in one hand and the glass in the other. "Whew! I'm thirsty," she says, and takes a big gulp.

"Honey, slow down. I want to give a toast." Nora uncorks the wine bottle, fills the glasses, and gives one to each of the men.

"To Christmas Eve," she says raising her glass, smiling.

"Christmas Eve!" they all say, raising their glasses as if love really will conquer all. Even Paul cheers. He is beginning to relax now, in this moment. He's untucked his shirt, extended his long legs on the ottoman, kicked off his shoes.

Fiona slams her glass on the coffee table. "Mommy! What time is it?"

"Fiona! Be careful!" Nora glances at the clock over the fireplace. "It's five minutes to midnight."

Fiona, her eyes wide and bright, turns to Stephen. "When it's midnight, everyone opens a present."

"How wonderful," he says with a grin. He picks up a sugar cookie from the plate, breaks it in half, and offers the other half to James.

Nora can understand why James is crazy about this man. She thinks about how things can change on a dime, how last Christmas, James sat in that exact place on the couch, his heart aching with loneliness. She remembers too how later that night, she and James had been out on the sidewalk, gazing in the window at the glittering tree, she'd been so comforted to have him there, but then he'd said, "I think we should search for Dad."

They'd had an argument then. He hadn't understood her, hadn't understood how much their father's disappearance had made her doubt herself. "My God," she'd whispered to him, even though they were alone on the street, "Who would leave their children and never come back? Especially when their mother had just died! Who would do that? And who lets his wife beat the crap out of their child?"

But James was too angry to hear her. "God, you're as cold as Mom! You know how the war fucked him up. Can't you ever just cut him some slack?" And then, out of nowhere, "Jesus, do you and Paul ever touch?" She'd walked away from him then, heard him yell, "Screw it! I'll look for Dad myself!"

James had gone home the next day, a week early. He'd waited until all the presents had been opened, waited until after Christmas dinner, for Fiona's sake. Nora and James had acted as if things were okay, they'd arranged their words carefully, sorted and organized their thoughts before speaking. And when he'd said goodbye, he'd kissed her, thanked her, and she'd hugged him back, but up close to him, she'd seen his eyelids, puffed and red, like he'd been crying.

And then, on New Year's Eve, he'd called her. "I'm not going to look for the bastard," he'd said.

"You're right. Who the hell would do those things?"

In the distance the cathedral chimes midnight. "It's time!" Fiona shouts, her face shining, as she rushes to the tree. She goes straight to a large box wrapped in bright red paper, marked "The Brown Family" in purple letters. She brings the gift over to Nora and sets it in her lap.

"It's for all of us! But who's it from?" Fiona asks.

"It doesn't say," Nora says, turning the box around.

"Delivered yesterday," says Paul. "It was wrapped in brown paper, so I figured I could unwrap it."

"Was there a postmark?" Nora asks.

"Didn't think of looking."

"Did you keep the paper?"

"Jesus, Nora. No, I threw it the fire last night. What's the big deal? Probably just from a neighbor or someone."

"It's a Christmas mystery! Maybe it's from Santa!" Fiona says, nervously.

"Go ahead and open it!" James says.

Fiona takes the box from Nora, kneels on the rug, and rips off the red paper. Inside, there's a white box filled with four smaller boxes, side by side, wrapped in the same kind of red paper. Each is tied with a purple ribbon.

"They have names on them, and there's one for each of us!" Fiona exclaims, reading each name

63

mystery person must know James is an artist."

"Hmmm," Nora says, thinking Stephen might be the secret Santa.

Fiona pulls off the purple ribbon and unwraps the red paper.

"A princess wand!"

"Goes with your tiara," James says, smiling.

Fiona twirls over to Paul and taps him lightly on the head with the wand. "Daddy, you gave me the tiara. Are you the mystery giver?"

"I am not, but you will always be my little princess."

Paul's spoken these words, *my little princess,* to Fiona before, and Nora had heard them as an endearment, but in this moment the words send a shudder through her body which startles her.

Fiona skips back over to the two small boxes left and picks up Paul's gift. "Here, Daddy, it's your turn!" She holds it out to him but then wrinkles her nose. "I smell something," she says, sniffing the box. "This smells like dirt!"

"Hey, whose present is this?" Paul asks, taking the gift from her and unwrapping it. He lifts out a small cedar box. He holds it up so they can see the picture of a handsome military leader wearing an elaborate royal blue uniform, a triumphant expression on his face.

"What's it say, Daddy? Who is that funny man?"

"That, my darling, is Simon Bolivar, the great Venezuelan warrior." He lifts the lid. "And these

65

asks, twirling around, still enjoying her wand.

"Of course," Nora says, though of course she will not.

"She's a sweetheart," James says later, when they are alone in the kitchen. He is pouring more whiskey into his coffee. "Want it?" he asks her, holding the mug out to her. She takes it, sips a little. Heat rushes down her throat.

"You okay, Sis? You seem tense." He pours coffee into another mug, one that says BEST DAD EVER, and adds a large gulp of whiskey.

"Was the fairy book your idea?" she says. "Did you tell Stephen to buy this for me?"

"What? Stephen didn't send that box!"

She studies him carefully. "The gifts are from Dad," she says then, in a small, thin voice.

James is silent. Holding his coffee mug with two hands.

"Do you know where he is?" she asks, fear spreading through her veins.

"Jesus, Nora, if I did, don't you think I'd have told you?" He takes a sip of his Irish coffee, looks at her for a long moment, and says, "You know, Nora, maybe he just wants to make amends."

She walks into the living room then picks up the fairy book from the coffee table, opens the fireplace screen, and throws the book into the flames. Pieces of fairy wings burn and flutter up the chimney.

CHAPTER NINE
1965

Nora, still in her nightgown, runs barefoot down the stairs and into the kitchen where her mother cracks eggs into a cast-iron skillet. "Mommy!" Nora shouts. "The dead tree in our front yard grew flowers!"

"The tree wasn't dead," her mother says, lifting the edges of the eggs with the spatula. "It's a crabapple tree, sure 'n' that's how they look."

"Crabapples!" Nora says, happily. Just the word alone, *crabapples,* the way it pops and bounces in her mouth, makes her giggle. "Mommy, why are they called crabapples? Are they crabby and grouchy and mean?" she asks, laughing.

"Nora," her mother says, "will ye stop with the questions and set the table?"

"But, Mommy, can you eat them?"

Her mother turns to her, holding the spatula in the air. "Nora! No, you can't eat them. Now set the table!"

Nora is seven, and they've just moved from Chicago's south side to its outskirts because now her father is the vice president of the Bank of Chicago and because the colored people made her mother hysterical, made her shriek, "I won't be raising me children around niggers," made her threaten to take Nora and James back to Ireland for good. And though Nora didn't understand her mother's troubles, more than anything, she secretly hoped they *would* go back to Ireland. They traveled there only one month a year, and she missed her grandfather tremendously—missed their walks through bogs that smelled of dung and clover, missed fishing for brown trout and summer salmon, missed the times when he'd play jigs and reels on his accordion, his rough hands flying over the tiny buttons making her forget she was ever afraid of anything.

But her mother didn't take them away to Ireland—instead her husband bought her a house on five acres of land.

"Hey, what's all this about crabapples?" her father asks, coming into the kitchen, wearing a starched white shirt, green paisley tie, navy suit pants, and the black shoes Nora had polished the night before. He swoops her up and sets her on the counter so she can look directly into his eyes, which makes her feel like they are king and queen of their own island.

"They never grow up," Nora says, matter-of-factly, "and they grow out of ugly dead trees, and you can't even eat them."

She wraps her arms and bare legs around her father and examines his face to see if he is just as surprised about crabapples. She guesses not, as he begins to tickle her. "And you know what else?" he asks.

"What?" Nora says giggling, knowing for sure nobody is smarter than her father.

"There's a song about crabapples." And he sings then, in his church voice, a voice so big Nora can feel it inside herself. *"Crabapples, crabapples, out in the wood, little and bitter, yet little and good!"*

He lifts Nora up and twirls her around the kitchen, singing, *"The apples in orchards, so rosy and fine, are children of wild little apples like mine."*

But then, her mother's voice. "Karl! For God's sake, stop!" Maeve doesn't like it when Karl acts silly, which seems enormously unfair to Nora. Her mother never uses the Lord's name in vain when her father plays with James.

Karl sets Nora on her chair, which is right next to his, straightens his tie, and sits down at the table.

"Is that the whole song, Daddy?" Nora asks, hugging her knees to her chest.

Her father winks and puts a finger to his lips to quiet her so they won't further aggravate her mother. He whispers, *"One little apple I'll catch for myself. I'll stew it and strain it to store on a shelf."*

"James, breakfast!" her mother shouts, carrying the pan of eggs to the table. James clamors down the stairs and into his chair. He has two plastic army men, one in each fist, and begins making them fight each other on his plate, shouting, *"Pow! Pow! Pow!"* until one of the soldiers falls dead into his eggs, and James giggles so hard he falls off his chair.

"Nora, put your knees down," her mother says then and pushes an egg roughly onto Nora's plate with the spatula, breaking the yolk, even though she knows how much Nora likes to poke the egg open herself and let the yellow out slow, slow, slow onto her toast.

Nora's heart bangs with anger, and she lets her mother know it by humming the new song and not putting her knees down either.

"Put your knees down," her mother says, her voice quiet, the kind of quiet that makes James go quiet, the kind of quiet that means she will knock you into the furniture as soon as Daddy goes to work, but Nora keeps humming, jabbing the deflated egg over and over with her fork.

"Nora," her father says softly, buttering his toast.

"Is that it?" Maeve asks, glaring at him. "She disobeys me and all you can say is 'Nora'?"

Sometimes Nora wishes her father would raise *his* voice to her mother, take charge, but mostly he just takes Nora aside before he leaves for work and says, "Now, Nora, be a good girl, and don't get your mother's Irish up today."

He'd told her once that her mother couldn't help it when her Irish came up because a long time ago the Irish people were treated meanly, and since then, most Irish children, especially the red-headed ones (like her mother) were born with a temper. Nora worries she herself has a temper even though her hair is blonde because once when she was angry she'd thrown her doll across the room at the dresser and didn't even try to fix her for days. She'd felt so bad about this she told Father Donahue at confession the following Saturday. The priest said throwing a doll was only a venial sin, not a mortal sin, because of the doll not being a real person. He told her to say ten Hail Marys as penance and to not do it again because a person who frequently indulges in venial sin is likely to collapse into mortal sin. When she'd asked the priest what *"collapse into mortal sin"* meant, he'd told her it was one step closer to ending up in hell.

From that day on, Nora worried so much about collapsing into mortal sin that when she felt even a hint of her Irish rising up, she hid in her closet until the temper went away.

But now Maeve's Irish is up, and she yanks Nora by her arm and throws her away from the table. "Get outside. Now."

Nora runs to the screen door, kicks it open, and lets it bang LOUD behind her. She runs to the crabapple tree and wraps her arms around it, tears streaming down her cheeks.

And now, the sound of the screen door banging again, and she watches her father trudge with his briefcase to the garage. He is not going to look for her. He gets into his car, starts the engine, and backs up slowly. When he is next to her, he rolls the window down and calls, "Princess, it'll be okay. I promise."

She runs to him then, stands on her bare tip-toes and grips the bottom of the window frame with her small hands. The cold steel of the car presses through her cotton nightgown.

"Daddy, please don't go. Please don't leave me. Please, Daddy."

"I'll be home soon, princess," he says, and he removes her fingertips from the window frame, puts his foot on the gas, and backs out of the driveway, leaving her there.

CHAPTER TEN
JANUARY 24, 1997

"It sounds like you were close to your father," David says, taking off his glasses and cleaning them with the hem of his brown cardigan. It's been a month since she's seen him. She'd canceled two appointments, hadn't felt she needed his help, hadn't heard voices, hadn't seen any floating faces. Even after throwing *The Crabapple Fairy* in the fire and realizing her father was still out there somewhere, she'd been okay, managed just fine. But lately, the anxiety was creeping back in, stealing her sleep, making her hard to get along with, making her pretend things—smiling while Fiona poured Cheerios and milk into her bowl, spilling half of it all over the table, and biting her tongue when she watched the evening news with Paul, him flipping channels and cursing at Clinton's inauguration and Albright's confirmation as first female secretary of state.

And so here she is. She's told David about the fairy book and the crabapple tree. She stares at the window even though the blinds are shut, the flattened metal slats thick with dust. Yes, she had been close to her father. For years she'd thought of nothing but him, but then he had deserted her, left her suspicious and suspended between truth and reality. The angry fist of her heart begins to pummel her chest. He is twenty-seven years too late.

"Tell me what you remember."

Her father's hands on the wires of his cello. Music in their house on Sundays. Brahms and Beethoven and Mozart through the walls and ceiling. And sometimes his mouth on a harmonica. Once, a buddy of his from the war, Clem, came to visit. At dinner Clem told them how her father had played the harmonica in the barracks at night. "Soothed us low and smooth to sleep," Clem said. "Low and smooth like cream." Her father's blue eyes had looked at his pork chops then, shy and quiet.

She pulls the raven pillow onto her lap, folds her hands on the raven's wings. "He was a good businessman, I think. A vice president at Bank of Chicago." She finds the zipper on the pillow and slowly zips and unzips it. Zip. Unzip. Zip. "And he had lots of friends. They'd come over on Saturday nights and drink scotch and play poker at the kitchen table once James and I were in bed." Zip. Unzip. Zip. "He told us once how he was an only child, how lonely he was, how his parents died young in a car accident and he went to Marymount Military Academy in Tacoma because an uncle recognized his musical talent and Marymount had one of the finest music programs."

Nora became aware that she was zipping and unzipping the pillow fast. She released it, tossed it to the other end of the couch. "He helped out a lot at church too—built a new sign and fixed the cross once when it broke in a tornado. The priest told me once how lucky I was to have such a kind father."

"Did you feel lucky?"

Heat creeps into her face and crouches there. Sweat drips under her breasts.

"Yes," she says, focusing on her folded hands. "Until he disappeared. I loved him more than anyone—until he disappeared." It is difficult to say this aloud, and she wishes she still had the pillow to hold.

"I'm sorry," David says.

"Anyway," she says and shrugs.

"Nora," he says, his voice soft. "Would you look at me for a moment?"

A slant of sun has slipped through a crack in the blinds, and she watches it light up his white hair. Another streak of light from a different crack stripes across his beard.

"What would you do if you ran into him on the street?" David asks. From the hallway the sound of a door slamming makes her jump. Her father could be right outside this building. And she is not ready. She is not ready to face the cauterized truth of him.

It is then that Nora sees the same disturbing

twist in the air that blurred her vision in the classroom, in the hotel. She blinks, blinks, blinks rapidly to bring David's face into her line of vision.

"Stay with the feeling," David is saying. "Stay with the feeling, Nora. You are safe," but it's becoming difficult to hear him and she is going away and a gauzy curtain unrolls slowly, slowly from the ceiling and it is floating, floating between them, swaying there and now she is fading, fading like a memory into silence. Her eyes close.

"Just let go," he says, sounding farther and farther away. "Let go. I'm right here. You are safe."

She lets go.

And now a huge startling movement in her head, as if a sliding door has opened along her cerebral cortex, a continental shift from her left hemisphere to the right. She opens her eyes.

"Nora, can you hear me?"

"I am Margaret," says a tiny voice.

"Nora?"

Margaret's heart is banging, banging.

"Nora, is that you?"

"I am Margaret."

"Margaret?"

"Please. Move away from me."

David moves to the green chair by the window. "How's that?" he says.

Now she doesn't know what to say. He is acting very nice.

He asks softly, "Margaret, why are you here?"

Silence.

She wants to talk to him. She wants to tell him things.

"How old are you, Margaret?"

"Six."

"Six. Well, Margaret, is there something you'd like to tell me?"

Margaret pulls her knees up to her chest and wraps her arms around them. She hides her face on her knees. She will be in big trouble now. She is not supposed to talk to anyone.

"It's all right. You are safe," he says.

She says nothing.

"Margaret?" he says. "Hello?" And then, a bit louder, "Nora?"

From a distance Nora hears David calling her name. She opens her eyes, slowly, her lids heavy. She is disoriented, the way one feels upon waking up in a hotel room. The kind of hotel room you stay in at the last minute because nothing else is available.

"Nora," David says gently. "Just breathe."

She fixes her eyes on him, and after a few moments, remembers where she is, who he is. He looks worried. She realizes her arms are wrapped around her knees, which are folded into her chest, and a ripple of confusion shoots through her. She

78

thrusts her feet to the ground and folds her hands on her lap, trembling.

After a long silence he says, carefully, "What are you feeling?"

"I . . . I . . . I don't know." She brings her shaking hand up to her cheek, touches it as if she is unsure she exists.

"You're okay. Take some deep breaths."

Nora looks at him and shudders. Through chattering teeth she asks, "Why are you sitting over there?"

"You asked me to move," he says, and she can see he is struggling to be careful with his words.

"What are you talking about?" she asks in a whisper.

"The words . . . of a little girl were coming from you." He pauses as if he is waiting for some sort of reaction from her. "She didn't want me near her, so I moved over here."

Nothing feels real. "She? What? What are you talking about?"

Again he says, "You spoke in the voice of a little girl . . . Nora, did you hear anything she said?"

"No, I didn't fucking hear anything." Nora rocks back and forth. She is close to tears. This is the moment she's worried about. The moment when the neurons in her brain misfire into complete chaos and it's too late to do anything about it. She should have taken medication to hold them together long before this, and now it's probably too late.

"Listen, whoever she is, she needed to speak, and you had the courage to allow her to do so."

"What the hell are you saying? How could you let this happen?" Nora says, her voice rigid with anger and fear. She stops rocking and pushes deeper into the back of the couch, clenching the pillow to her chest. Her mind is a collision, a multivehicle accident. No survivors.

He moves to his usual chair, faces her directly. "You are allowing yourself to remember something. I believe *she* is assisting you." He says all of this as if he says it every day, to everyone, to anyone who sits on his couch.

"Do you hear yourself?" Nora whispers.

"She *is* you, Nora."

"She *is* me? What the hell are you talking about?" She shakes her head in disbelief that something this bizarre could be happening to her.

The tears come then, a burst of sobs, huge and consuming, her shoulders lurching up and down, and she can't breathe, and she chokes on the swallowed tears, and David won't stop saying, "Breathe, Nora, breathe," and she would strangle him if she could, breathe if she could, but she's drowning and she can't remember if she's cried like this before, and then her grandfather's words in her ear, *You are tough, you are stronger than you think,* and she catches her breath, and now the tears diminish into a few short, quick breaths and slowly, finally, come to a stop.

"This is difficult. I know. But we will figure this out," David says leaning toward her, his face serious, his hands folded on his knees.

"We'll figure this out?" she gasps out, her throat tight. "What am I supposed to do now? Go home?" She pauses, needing to swallow. "What if I go crazy at home?" she whispers and then rocks back and forth, bringing her hands to her face, covering her wet cheeks. All she wants is to curl up into a little ball, climb under something, and melt into oblivion.

"Nora. Stop. You're scaring yourself. If I for a minute, for even a minute, thought you weren't safe leaving here, I wouldn't send you home."

Nora isn't sure what to think. "Is this—shit, like *Sybil*?"

"The case portrayed in *Sybil* was extremely severe—and rare, perhaps less than .01 percent of the general population. Dissociation occurs along a continuum and is part of the range of normal experience. Nora, it is far too early to speculate about what is happening for you and where this falls on that spectrum." He stops for a moment, looks at her gently, as if giving her time to assimilate what he'd said. When she says nothing, only continues to bite her lip, he says, "It seems to me that your brain is working hard to remember something. If we could somehow connect with that past wiring, the past memories, we could understand how to rewire the pathways so your brain could be healthy again. But look, this is a lot for today. I think you should rest, process this, and we'll talk about it more next time—"

"I'm going home," Nora says then, without making an effort to stand.

"Please, rest for a minute. It will be okay. Can you come in tomorrow—Saturday?"

She stands up, but her legs are useless with shaking, and she sits back down.

"Nora? Did you hear me? Can you meet Saturday?" he stands up and walks over to his desk. He moves his index finger down the calendar page. "How about 10:00 a.m.? Will that work?"

She nods her head and stands again, more steadily now. She pulls on her coat and opens the door. The cold startles her.

"See you tomorrow," he says.

She rushes out, toward home, rushes down the dark street, past the glittering bookstores and coffee shops, past the Space Needle with its weird alien suggestions, past the stutter and stammer of rush hour traffic. All the way home she thinks, *This can't be happening. God! How does this happen to a person?*

Finally, here is her home. She almost can't bear to look at it. The weight of it. A 1930s red brick bungalow with ivy growing up the chimney. A red brick path edged in purple hydrangeas leads to the bright red door. She was twenty-three, he was twenty-eight when they moved in. The first night he'd officially carried her over the threshold, turned the key to unlock the brown door (they'd painted it a week later), and they'd shared a pepperoni pizza and Coors beer on the renovated wood floor in the living room. They'd talked about furniture and future plans (no children for at least three years) and where to put the recycling bins. They'd felt like grown-ups. Now the house gazes back at her as if she is a stranger, as if it's observing her, deciding if she is worthy of entrance.

"I'm back," she says, standing in the doorway of Paul's study, feeling blurred and insecure.

"Fiona's in bed," he says indifferently, keeping his eyes on his computer, his back toward her. Next to him: a plate with crumbs and a balled-up paper napkin, a trace of whiskey in a glass.

"Still working on the Lincoln Plaza?" she asks, pangs of guilt now.

"Still? Do you know how long a deal like this takes? This is the biggest project Bellevue's seen in a decade! Do you know what it means if I land this?"

She does know. Points on his scorecard. He needs to stay at the top of the heap. Like her father. She pictures her father then, decades ago, sitting in the kitchen, papers and files arranged in neat piles around him. She'd sit across from him working out math problems or writing a story. Her mother washing dishes. The quiet way her mother had wiped her hands on a towel, hesitated by the table, then asked her father to take a walk, take a minute away from his work. The way her father had looked at her mother, exasperated. As if she was stupid. The way he'd said, "This deal will put me on the map, Maeve. On the map."

Nora leaves Paul and walks up the stairs to her daughter's bedroom. Fiona snoring softly, one arm under her head, another around her stuffed orca. Nora bends down and kisses her on the cheek, her skin a flower blossom. She sits in the rocking chair by Fiona's bed. This chair was the first thing she'd purchased when she'd become pregnant. She remembers the deep sense of responsibility she'd felt placing the chair in Fiona's bedroom. Her first normal, motherly thing. She'd sat in the chair, on the polished wood, her hands pressed upon her pregnant belly, and she'd known happiness then. Intense happiness. And she had nursed Fiona in this chair, lullabied her to sleep in it, Fiona's murmurings intertwining so magically with her own. A sane mother rocking her baby to sleep.

"Nora?" Paul's voice from the bedroom brings her back, makes her aware she is rocking fast and hard in the chair. She hadn't heard him come up the stairs.

"Have you seen my gray Nike sweatshirt?"

She stands and walks into the bedroom, sits on the edge of the bed. "No," she says, wearily. She hears him rummage through hangers.

"God, this place is a shit hole!"

"Sorry. But Paul?"

"What?" He is more irritated lately. He emerges from the closet with three gray sweatshirts and stands looking at her for several moments before holding each of the shirts up and inspecting their logos. He finds the Nike, pulls it over his head, and walks to the mirror. He speaks to her in the reflection. "Christ, you look terrible. I thought therapy was supposed to make you feel better."

She knows he is frustrated, scared—he's not prepared to be married to a crazy person.

"Paul, in the session today, I—"

He turns around and walks over to his dresser, opens the second drawer, and grabs a pair of fresh socks. For the few seconds it takes him to pull them on, she changes her mind. She still can't tell him about the voice. It wouldn't do any good to talk about it right now. Not with this hostility between them and not when she herself doesn't even know what is real and what is not.

"I'm going to head over to Mahoney's and watch the game, have a beer."

"Fine." But then she notices that he's freshly shaven, something he never does before going to Mahoney's. He's lying.

Once he's gone, she walks downstairs, her hand on the railing, to the kitchen, where she swallows spoonful after spoonful of artificially sweetened vanilla ice cream.

CHAPTER ELEVEN
THE MORNING OF JANUARY 25, 1997

It is Saturday. Fiona stands barefoot on a wooden stool at the kitchen counter in her favorite flannel nightgown, the one with the bluebirds on it, mixing pancake batter. Paul, still wearing the same clothes from the night before, (he must have slept on the couch) holds the large red bowl steady for her. The Sonics game blares from the radio, and Paul is shouting at Payton to "Run, damn it! Pass! Get off your damn knees!"

"Yeah!" Fiona yells, "Get off your damn knees!"

"Paul, can I talk to you for a moment?" Nora calls from the doorway. "In the living room?"

"I'll keep listening, Daddy," Fiona says. "I'll tell you what happens."

Paul follows Nora into the living room and flops on the couch, his arm over his eyes. She sits on the opposite end, near his feet.

She stares at his feet then and realizes she has never kissed his body from head to foot like you read about in the magazines, see in the movies. She's never even squirted whipped cream on his toes or fingers or anywhere and sucked it off. An unexpected thorn of failure stabs at her, even though, in fifteen years of marriage, he has never asked for whipped cream, has never voiced those kinds of needs, those kinds of desires. But maybe now he's had a change of heart, maybe now he wants more. Of course he wants more. She considers shouting, "DO YOU WANT ME TO SQUIRT WHIPPED CREAM ON YOUR BODY? ARE YOU HAVING AN AFFAIR?" She isn't prepared for a fight though, doesn't have the energy, feels she needs to reserve her fortitude for putting herself back together again. Instead she says, "David wants to see me this morning."

"Why?" Paul asks, almost angry, making her aware she is the one changing the rules.

"I don't know," she lies.

"But on a Saturday?" Paul says, sitting up, his hair and clothes rumpled and sideways. "Look at this place."

She looks. Looks at the messy living room: Christmas cards still on the fireplace mantle, most of them tipped over, pine needles scattered on the wood floor (Paul had taken the tree to the curb weeks ago), Fiona's stuffed animals strewn around. A naked Barbie doll facedown on the floor near a half-eaten peanut butter sandwich on a paper plate. Morning light slanting through the window magnifies soft piles of dust in every corner.

"What's happened to you?" he says. He stands and picks up the paper plate, folds it in half and then in half again, the sandwich squished inside it. "You used to be meticulous. You used to care." Something catches in his voice then, and she thinks he might cry.

She jumps up and grabs the Barbie doll, begins to collect the stuffed animals. "Oh, Paul, I'm sorry, I—" but then a shriek, a loud thump from the kitchen. "Shit!" Nora gasps, drops the toys, and runs into the kitchen, Paul close behind.

A white-faced Fiona sits on the floor, the flames of the propane stove high.

Fiona rubs her elbow, eyes welling. Paul rushes to turn off the stove, and Nora goes to Fiona, kneels down by her, moves her bangs from her eyes. "What happened? Are you okay?"

"I turned on the stove, and the fire scared me, and I fell off the stool."

"Here, stand up, sweetheart, let's be sure you're okay."

Fiona stands for a moment then wiggles her body in place. "I'm okay, Mommy."

Paul draws in a slow deep breath, turns off the radio, says, "Sweetie. Don't ever, ever do that again. You could have been burned very badly."

"I'm sorry, Daddy, I wanted to help. I wanted—" but then she bursts into sobs, sits down on the floor, blonde head in small hands.

"What is it, honey?" says Nora, stroking Fiona's hair. "Did you want to show us you're a big girl?"

"No . . . I . . . I wanted to make you . . . and Daddy breakfast so . . . you would be happy . . . and . . ."

"And what?" Paul says, gentler now.

"And like each other again."

Over the top of Fiona's head, Paul's eyes meet Nora's with a look of guilt that shoots straight from his heart into hers.

"How are you feeling?" David asks her once he is settled back to listen and she has adjusted the raven pillow on her lap, folded her hands on its wings, careful to leave the black of its eye exposed. Her grandfather told her once that ravens were omniscient, the wisest of all animals. "There is wisdom in a raven's head," he'd say whenever one flew over the house.

"Nora?"

"I'm afraid," she says quietly.

"I understand."

"I wasn't expecting this."

"No one expects this."

"My body feels strange to me," she says. She focuses her eyes on the closed window blinds. "And Fiona knows something is wrong." She pauses for a moment. Outside, someone revs the engine of a car. The ferry horn blows in the distance, and she wishes she were on it, wishes she were gazing out at whitecaps and gulls and islands instead of grimy metal blinds. "I'm scared we'll mess her up for life." And then, "Shit, I'm so fucked up."

"You aren't fucked up, and you're not going to mess Fiona up for life." He studies her eyes as if he's deciding whether or not to continue. "Listen—and Nora, you do have to know, I'm not someone who adheres closely to labels, but you may be suffering from post-traumatic stress disorder—PTSD—it's a condition triggered by something horrible, and the symptoms can be flashbacks, nightmares, anxiety, hallucinations, and so on."

Thoughts of soldiers returning from war without arms or legs or hope come into her mind. She leans back into the couch and stares at the ceiling. No one says anything for several minutes.

"Dissociation—an altered state of consciousness—is on the PTSD continuum. People sometimes dissociate when they fear death or can't escape a dangerous situation—they mentally leave the situation, imagine they're somewhere else, lose awareness of the environment, become someone else. Some may see the event as happening to someone else and watch as if they're a bystander. Many try to forget the event and contain the memories in a mental lockbox in order to keep functioning in a normal way."

She continues to stare at the ceiling. It is

beginning to be difficult to track all the words. She feels a bit like she's listening underwater.

"Are you with me?" he says.

"Mmmhmm."

"It's possible your mind pushed a trauma into a corner of your subconscious, and now the memory is coming through—through the altered consciousness of the voice you are hearing."

She resurfaces, though her eyes stay fixed on the ceiling. "Why? Why now? Why a voice?"

"I don't know. No one really knows—though there is certainly a lot of speculation—"

"Like what? What kind of speculation?"

"Well, for example, sometimes when your child reaches an age that was difficult for you as a child, sometimes . . . things are relived. And the fact that both she and Fiona are six, well, there might be something to this. But what we do know is that at its root is extreme stress, trauma."

"Oh, my God," she says, looking at him now. "Here we go again with the trauma. Did you even hear me when I said I haven't been traumatized—at least anything near enough to cause this?"

"Yes, I heard you. Listen, I'm not sure why this aspect of you, this little girl, would need to speak. I just know that whatever is hidden in the subconscious will struggle to reveal itself. You have basically been keeping a secret from yourself all this time."

She stares at him, unblinking, rocking gently back and forth.

"And again, for the record, your mother beating you and dying in front of you is pretty serious." He pauses. "And your father abandoning you when you were eleven is no small thing either."

She says nothing for a moment. Those things are in the past, and except for the last few months, she's been able to leave them there. "Do I seem like someone who's been traumatized?"

"Nora, trauma survivors respond in different ways. They may do well in one area but not in another. They may function well at work but not in personal relationships. They may be great parents but have a debilitating addiction. I don't know what to tell you. It's just too early in the process."

"Shit," she says, forcing herself to stop rocking. "I can't believe this, I really can't believe this."

"Dissociation is a *normal* response to an abnormal situation. It's a way of coping. We'll figure this out."

"What did she—the voice—say?" Nora asks, finally.

"She only said a few words. She seemed very in control but very scared. She didn't want me to look at her, and when I turned away, she was gone."

She stares at him for a moment. "But what did she say?"

"She told me her name."

Shock breaks across her face like a slap. "She has a name?"

"Yes."

"What is it?"

"Margaret."

Margaret. Nora's heart pummels her chest. *Margaret.*

Then, images: A book. A book with a purple velvet cover and a gold lettered title, *St. Margaret.* A crown. A sword. A dead dragon. Sister Rosa.

Nora hears David calling her name and slowly opens her eyes.

"What is it, Nora?" he asks.

Nora gets her bearings, stammers, "I . . . I need to go—I'll call you," she says and runs out of the room.

CHAPTER TWELVE
JANUARY 25, 1997

Nora has an hour before she is expected home. She will walk, pull herself together, insist herself into a calmer state. She doesn't know why images of Sister Rosa, the dragon, and the book of St. Margaret have materialized in her mind. They must have meaning, must have something to do with *"Margaret,"* but what? And how are they related to the Valentine's dress? She remembers so little about that time in her life, rarely thinks about it—but she needs to try and remember, to sort this out.

The day is cold, and she wraps her arms around herself to push away the chill, a chill magnified by apprehension flailing like a trapped sparrow in her chest. Up ahead, in Pike Place Market, there's a Starbucks, and she thinks she might feel better if she has something to eat. A croissant maybe, or a blueberry muffin and a latte. She enters, orders three croissants (she will bring two home, one for Paul and one for Fiona) and a nonfat decaffeinated cappuccino. "You mean a 'double nothing,'" the young barista named Clive says, and she nods, smiles a bit—the first time in days. She asks for a pat of butter and strawberry jam. The coffee shop is crowded but quiet, filled with people who seem content and sleepy, relieved it's Saturday. Billie Holiday plays in the background, and Nora feels a little more in control now.

She finds a table way in the back with a single chair. She sits down, sets the coffee and white bag on the table, and stares at them. The fat from the croissants seeps through the bag, and she thinks maybe she isn't hungry after all. She takes out her notebook and a pencil and begins to sketch a picture of Sister Rosa, her old teacher, the one who made them stop and pray a Hail Mary every time a siren zoomed by the school. Nora is startled at how easily the details come to her: the black veil with its stiff white wimple tightly wrapping Sister Rosa's round face, escaped wisps of black hair in such contrast to the bleached linen; the loose black dress draping to the ground, wooden rosary beads clipped to little hooks on a black woven belt, a large silver crucifix hanging from a black cord around her neck, the simple silver wedding ring on her left hand, the functional black shoes.

Nora draws question marks in the spaces, traces the outline of Sister Rosa over and over. Then, her hand, the one holding the pencil, suddenly feels like it belongs to someone else. She watches as the hand writes: *Everyone has their own way of being brave.* And then she remembers these are Sister Rosa's words—she'd said them to Nora at the convent. The hand puts the pencil down then, takes a croissant from the bag, butters it, smears the jam into the butter, and shoves it into Nora's mouth. The mouth eats it all very quickly and wants more. The hand feeds the mouth another croissant, and the eyes close.

Nora is in first grade at St. Raphael's Catholic School in Illinois. She is marching through deep snow in oversized red boots from the school to the convent. It is her job during lunch recess to bring a carton of milk from the school cafeteria to the nuns. She counts her steps as she marches. She tries to make it in exactly 256 steps. Sometimes she has to make giant steps toward the end of the path, or it would go over 256. The day is cold, but the sun is strong and the sky a bright blue. A light wind lifts new snow from old snow, and the flakes swirl around her, and she feels like a body in a snow globe.

Sometimes Sister Rosa invites her into the library and reads her a book.

"I like this one," Nora whispers, holding a book with a picture of a beautiful woman riding a white horse on the cover.

"That's a book about St. Margaret," Sister Rosa says, kneeling next to her.

"Why does she have a sword?"

"St. Margaret dedicated her life to protecting those in danger. When she was little, her mother died, and her father gave her to a shepherdess in the country. Margaret spent her days watching over the lambs. While she was tending the lambs, she would pray her rosary. Later, when her father found out she was dedicating her life to God, he became angry, and she had to leave their home, and she went off to protect those who were in danger."

Nora traces Margaret's sword with her finger while Sister Rosa speaks.

"And once she stood in front of a dragon with her sword raised in one hand and the cross of her rosary raised in the other, and the dragon lost all its powers."

"Why does she have a pearl necklace on her head?"

"That's her crown. The name Margaret comes from the Greek word for 'pearl.' "

"I wish I was brave like St. Margaret," Nora says.

"Why must you be brave sweetheart? You're only a child."

Nora's eyes begin to blink rapidly then and well up, and now she is crying jagged sobs that hit the walls and shatter into tiny pieces on the rug and disappear.

Sister Rosa leans forward and gently tries to bring Nora onto her lap, but Nora pushes her away.

"Don't . . . Don't . . ." Nora says between sobs. She wipes at her eyes with her sweater sleeve, stands up, and walks toward the front door.

"Wait," Sister Rosa calls, following her. As Nora struggles to pull on her boots, Sister Rosa walks to a little wooden table in the vestibule, opens the top drawer, and lifts out a crystal rosary, each bead an iridescent blue.

She kneels in front of Nora so their eyes are even, Nora's blue eyes still watery. Sister Rosa helps Nora button her coat and put on her mittens and says, "I know little girls usually receive this at their first communion, but I want you to have it now." Sister Rosa places the rosary in Nora's mittened hand and closes her fingers around it.

"Keep it in your pocket, and touch it whenever you need help. And Nora?"

"Yes, Sister?"

"You can call for St. Margaret to help you anytime."

"Thank you, Sister," Nora whispers. Sister Rosa opens the heavy door for her, and the cold air is sharp as Nora steps out. She looks back at Sister Rosa.

"Everyone has their own way of being brave," Sister Rosa says. Nora nods and marches back to school, retracing exactly 256 steps.

Nora's eyes open then, agitated and off-center. She blinks. The memory had arrived like a heart, pinkish-gray and pulsing, soft without edges. And now, relief: she has placed all the misplaced pieces—the book with the gold lettered title, *St. Margaret*; the crown; the sword; the dead dragon; Sister Rosa—into a whole! She did it! David was right about the trauma of her mother beating her, dying in front of her having an impact. She has remembered. She has remembered and now she can move on. She is relieved, pleased.

She licks the crumbs off her lips. With a napkin, she wipes the greasy remnants from the table into her other hand and dumps them into the white bag and folds the bag closed, squishes it, with the one croissant still left inside, into a ball. She will buy new croissants. Around her, people are still drinking coffee and reading things from the newspaper out loud to each other. Life is moving on. She stands, but then she freezes. Here is Paul in his green winter parka and wool hat standing at the counter. Paul is standing there ordering things, and he is holding Fiona's hand, and next to Fiona is a pretty woman wearing a Seahawks cap. The woman is touching Fiona's shoulder, touching Fiona's red coat, smiling big white teeth, and Fiona smiling back, shyly.

Nora's heart stops and her face grows hot and the room is thick as a dark forest. She watches the barista give each of them a cup with a lid. Fiona holds the cup with both mittened hands and blows into the little hole in the lid. The woman and Paul look at each other with open affection, and then the trio exits, Paul smiling and holding the door open for the woman and Fiona.

The hand takes the third croissant out of the white paper bag and breaks it into little pieces and feeds it to the ravenous mouth.

"What did you two do this morning?" Nora asks, falsely nonchalant, once the three of them are sitting together at home, eating grilled cheese sandwiches. She wants to see how Paul responds, a part of her hoping the attraction she witnessed was imagined.

"Not much," Paul shrugs, his casual tone as exaggerated as her own.

"We went for a walk with Elisa, and we drank hot chocolate in the park," Fiona says cheerfully, unaware of life's complexities.

"Elisa?" Nora says, adrenaline beginning to pump, and she isn't sure she won't start crying.

"You know her, Mommy—the lady who plays the violin—the lady next door."

"Christ, can you lighten up?" Paul says later, after Fiona has gone off to the playground with her friend, Sarah.

"She touched Fiona," Nora whispers, clenching her coffee cup until her knuckles are white.

"Nora! Come on! It was hot chocolate. It didn't mean a thing."

"It goddamn means a thing to me!" she shrieks,

and now the mug is flying through the air, a visible obscenity, hitting the refrigerator and shattering into bits at Paul's feet.

"You're crazy," he yells, grabbing his coat from the hall closet, walking out, slamming the door.

"Bastard!" she shouts.

And when Sarah's mother calls to ask if Fiona can spend the night, "The girls are having so much fun!" Nora is relieved and climbs into bed with her clothes on. And when she hears Paul come home at 3:00 a.m. and walk unsteadily to the living room couch, she closes her eyes and tries not to think about where he's been.

CHAPTER THIRTEEN
JANUARY 27, 1997

"Sister Rosa sounds lovely," David says, his face expectant as a blank page. He is dressed in jeans and a rumpled shirt with rolled-up sleeves, his hair as rumpled as his shirt. Suddenly she wants to kiss him. Even though he is old enough to be her father, she wants to devour him, get lost in him, lose herself in him. Startled by this urge, the transparent cliché of it, she turns away, embarrassed, tries to clear her mind of it, but ends up closing her eyes and imagining the intimate perfection of his lips on hers.

"Nora? Are you with me?"

She opens her eyes, confused and flustered. The image gone, dissolved, defunct. The reality of her cracked life back, her past a malevolent undertow she cannot escape from simply by swimming parallel to and waiting for release; no, this is a force demanding a surrender she cannot allow.

She sits guiltily, hoping her dreaming, her lust, will not be evident. She thinks of how she must look: dark jeans, black T-shirt, heavy black Doc Martens shoes, all of it overtly unfeminine, undeniably hands-off. Of course he wouldn't desire her. She hears then the small clock on the cabinet next to her, ticking, ticking, ticking. She clenches and unclenches her fists.

"Nora?"

She needs the clock to stop ticking.

"Nora?"

"It's . . . the clock," she says. "It's the ticking—"

"I'll move it," David says. He rises, picks up the clock and places it in the bottom drawer of his desk across the room, and sits back down.

"Paul looked like he was in love," she says.

"You mean when you saw him at the coffee shop?"

"Yeah."

"Do you want to talk about that?"

She doesn't know what to talk about. She is conscious her thoughts are lurching and spinning and fear is creeping in with its jagged edges and she works hard now to reassure herself she is fine, but she is not succeeding. She wants him to take charge, tell her what to say and do.

"Nora?"

"Sister Rosa told me to pray to Saint Margaret if I was scared. Why would she say that? I mean obviously, nuns tell you to pray to the saints, but she seemed to think I should specifically pray to St. Margaret. And now with the voice calling herself Margaret—" she can still hear that clock. She puts her hands over her ears and begins to rock back and forth slightly. "The clock," she whispers.

"Nora, it's okay. Here, I'll put it down the hall." He pulls the clock out of the drawer and leaves her there for a few moments. She presses her spine into the back of the couch and grabs the raven pillow and the room is so silent she can hear the ticking of her heart, a ticking that grows louder now, TICK TICK, mocking her, TICK TICK, you can't hide, TICK TICK—

"There, how's that?" David asks, back now, sitting down, once again on his chair, his voice not the least impatient.

She pulls the pillow up to her face. "One . . . two . . . three," she says, her heart going *bang* . . . *bang* . . . *bang*.

"Nora?" David says in a whisper.

"Four . . . five . . . six . . . seven . . . eight . . ."

"Margaret? Is that you?"

"Nine . . . ten . . . eleven . . . twelve . . ."

"Margaret? Can you talk to me?"

"Don't look at me," Margaret says into the pillow. She wants to go back inside, but it is her job to save Fiona.

"I'll move over here." He moves to the chair by the window.

He is nice, but she will be careful.

"Margaret, can you hear Nora?"

"Yes," she whispers. She is not used to talking out loud and it feels wrong and her tummy feels wrong.

"Margaret, are there others inside helping Nora?"

105

"No, it's just me." This is too many questions. She needs to go back in.

"Margaret, do you know anything about St. Margaret?"

She bites the side of her bottom lip and moves the pillow so there is a tiny space for air. She loves St. Margaret. She will tell him. "We have the same names and she fought a dragon and then the dragon swallowed her but she got out and then the dragon came back as a man and tried to trick her and she caught him by the head and threw him to the ground and put her foot on his neck and said, 'Lie still, thou fiend, under the feet of a woman.' " She peeks up for a moment, but then her face is back into the pillow. "Liar, liar, liar," she says.

"Margaret, who's a liar?"

"Liar, liar, liar," she says again, her voice making itself loud. She is mad at Nora. Very, very mad.

"Margaret, please, tell me. Who is a liar?"

"Nora . . . she . . . she prayed to Saint Margaret. A lot. Nora wanted Saint Margaret and then she made me and now she says she doesn't even know me!" Margaret forgets to be careful, forgets to hide her face. She looks at David's back. He is still looking at the window, so he is not mad with her. Then a man's voice from outside the door! It is him! A scream shoves out of her mouth.

"Margaret?" David swivels around in his chair.

She is curled up in the corner of the couch, her hands covering her face.

Silence fills the room.

"Margaret?"

Nora opens her eyes slowly, realizes her hands are covering her face. Tentatively, she brings her hands down, feeling lightheaded and jumbled. There is David across the room, observing her. She realizes her knees are up and quickly straightens them.

"When I came back from putting the clock away, Margaret was here," David says. He stops for a moment and glances at her uneasily, as if checking her ability to handle all this.

"And?" she says.

"Did you hear her?" he asks.

"No," she says with difficulty. Her mouth feels separate from her, unfaithful. "Why couldn't I? I can hear everything else." She is quiet for a moment, listening intently. "I can hear the gulls, the ferry horn, people out in the hall. I heard that goddamn clock hidden in a closed drawer. Why can't I hear her?"

"Each of these situations is different, Nora. Some people can hear the change, some cannot. Think about it like this: Assume your brain has one box holding all the stress in your life. That box is full; things are overflowing. In your attempt to keep order, you've created another container. That container holds Margaret and her memories. You've had a tight lid on that box—and now it's loose."

"Do you think there are others?" She's been thinking about Sybil since their last meeting. She'd seen the movie in college, and it had terrified her so much she'd left the theater, ran out on her date. Yesterday, she'd gone to the library to read about multiple personalities, but when she'd arrived at the mental health shelves she'd panicked. She'd stood there, blinking and disoriented, and then she'd walked over to the encyclopedias and read about St. Margaret. She'd read hundreds of saint stories in school, and their deaths always terrified her. All the flames and burning faces and sizzling hair and hearts and heads stabbed onto stakes and screams for mercy while thousands of faces watched. There were always faces watching.

But she read the article and looked for clues. Margaret was a girl who lived in Turkey in the early fourth century. Daughter of a pagan priest. Her mother passed on soon after her birth, and she was given to a woman who raised sheep out in the country. The woman raised Margaret in Christianity, which pissed off her father, who said she'd have to choose between religion and him. She chose the church. One day, a Roman wanted her to be his wife. Again, she said no. He was humiliated and had her arrested for being a Christian. When she wouldn't give up her faith, he tried to burn her, but the flames didn't hurt her. Then he tried to boil her in a cauldron of scorching water. As guards plunged her into the water, the heavens opened, and a snow-white dove flew down and placed a crown on Margaret's head. She stood up without any sign of burns. This, of course, angered the Roman even more, so he threw her into prison. Satan then visited her in the form of a dragon. The dragon swallowed her, but she stabbed his innards with her cross, and he spit her out. Finally, they chopped off her head. No one knows what happened to the blonde head of hers, but her hand is now under glass at the Vatopedi Monastery in Greece.

"Nora?"

She opens her eyes, though she doesn't remember closing them. Her heart is beating madly, and she is filled with rage. Rage for the faces who stood by and watched a still-alive woman burn to ash.

"Nora, what's going on?"

"I don't know," she snaps. "What the hell were we talking about?"

He leans forward. Looks at her intently, his brown eyes sharp and steady. "You asked if there might be others."

She takes a deep breath. Unclenches her fists. She is not angry with him. "Do you think there are?"

"I asked Margaret that—she says there are not,"

he says, his voice soft. "But we'll have to wait and see." He pauses for a moment. "It's really too early to know for sure."

"Too early to know for sure? Shouldn't you know *something* by now? God, are you even qualified for this type of problem?" She stares then at the certificate hanging on the wall, reads it aloud in an acrid tone, "David Forrester, MD, University of Wisconsin, Certified in Adult, Adolescent, and Child Psychiatry by the American Board of Psychiatry and Neurology."

She turns to him and says, "What does that really mean? That you're *certified* to save a screaming, slipping, cracked mind by nodding and saying, 'Mmmhmm,' repeatedly for a hundred bucks an hour?"

She can feel herself becoming cruel, but he is not unnerved, only looks at her calmly, like a parent managing a child going through a phase, which pisses her off even more. "You hardly seem worried at all. Are you so desensitized from listening to story after story of abuse and infidelity and messed-up human beings that you know there's nothing you can do anyway, that it's not your problem—" She stops then, glares at her shoes. *The anger. Christ, the anger.* Her pulse races, berserk as a rabid animal.

David gets up and walks to the window, opens the blinds a crack, looks through the slats. Sunlight stripes his face, neck, and chest.

"Look," he says, "if you decide to continue with me, I'm not going anywhere. No matter what. Do you hear me? I'm here for the long haul." He hesitates for a moment, turns, and looks hard at her, "And for the record, most of what I know comes from my life, not school. Don't you think for a moment I haven't had my share of hell." His face is so fervent she has to turn away, but the surprise of his admission, the intensity of it, has a strangely calming effect on her.

"And," he continues, "it *is* critical you work with someone you are comfortable with, so if you don't feel comfortable with me, we should find you someone else."

She looks at the certificate, the ceiling, the absoluteness of him. "I'll work with you," she says, finally, in a whisper.

He nods. "Good. And here's another truth—ultimately, you are the one who will save you. Not me. You. You'll have to work hard. Harder than you've ever worked on anything in your life. I can support you, advise you, but in the end, you are the one who will reconstruct the broken pieces, patch the cracks. You will make the choice to transcend this—whatever *it* is."

She pushes her hair back from her face. Tears spring to her eyes.

His voice is softer now. "You have what it takes, Nora. Just the fact you are here shows incredible strength. Very few people take this step, you know." He reaches for the tissue box near his chair and hands it to her.

She wipes the tears off her face. She wants to believe she has what it takes. She wants to believe she is not broken; she is fixable.

"Listen. I've had clients come to me who have had alternate personalities speak during sessions, but nowhere else. My concern would be much greater if Margaret took control of your life outside of this office—which leads to my next question."

He leans forward in his chair, clasps his hands together, taps his thumbs together a couple of times and says, "Have you ever felt that you blanked out and found yourself somewhere unexpected? Like you left for school but ended up in a department store and didn't know how you got there?"

She thinks for several moments, shakes her head no.

"Has anyone ever mentioned you were talking to yourself?"

She shakes her head again and says, "Well, maybe, but everyone talks to themselves a little, don't they?"

"Yes, of course, and like most things, this is on a continuum. But have people commented to you about it—your talking aloud to no one in particular?"

"No. No, they haven't."

She is silent for a long time. Until the last few weeks, she has always felt in control of her life. Perhaps not completely in control (look at the way she binges and starves, binges and starves) but she has always felt present. So okay, maybe she can relax now, maybe this *is* a temporary thing. This voice, this Margaret, is merely a part of her consciousness, that's all, a voice she'll work with in therapy, in this office. But now, new thoughts flash through her mind. What if Margaret shows up outside this office now that the cat's out of the bag? What if she shows up again at school?

Nora imagines herself standing in front of her class showing how adverbs can weaken a perfectly good sentence, when everything becomes blurry and her eyes close and Margaret appears and curls up on the floor and the students panic and call the administration. And here is John, running down the hall and bursting into the classroom door, seeing her, the Department Head of English, huddled up, skirt rolled around her waist, underwear on display, lips opening and closing, babbling things in a child's voice. The students staring; they are shocked, fascinated, disturbed. Some look away and then back again.

Or what if Paul sees Margaret? Puts a hand on her and she freaks? What if Fiona is watching? Nora sees Fiona there, the face and body of her, frozen. Oh, God. Paul will take her away forever.

All this *could* happen. A few months ago she would have said no, this could not happen, but now she knows it could. She whispers, "Do you think she'll speak outside of this office?"

"I don't know, Nora. I don't know. My sense is that she feels safe speaking here, with us, and if we help her it will stay that way."

"Why hasn't she spoken before? Why now?"

He shrugs. "Perhaps she was resting. You've said before how safe you felt with your grandparents, how lovely it was to live with them—my sense is she rested then. And perhaps this last fifteen years with Paul has been fairly uneventful, am I right? So perhaps something has happened lately—something has triggered her need to come out—or maybe she needed you to be at a place in your life where you could handle what she needs to say. Or maybe it's because she's the same age as Fiona. I'm not sure. I'm just not sure." He looks at his watch. "Nora, our session is almost over, and I haven't yet told you what Margaret said."

"Shit."

"If this feels like too much, I can tell you next time."

"No. Tell me now."

"She was very upset."

"*She's* very upset?" Nora says, a bit angrily.

David watches her, hesitates.

"Tell me."

"She said you prayed to St. Margaret and to use her words, she said you prayed to her *a lot*. And Nora," he says gently, almost like he is apologizing, "she said you are a liar."

"A liar? A liar? What the hell?" Nora feels haunted, deranged, violated, like a house that's burglarized and then the robber turns out to be someone you know.

CHAPTER FOURTEEN
THE EVENING OF JANUARY 27, 1997

When Nora arrives home, Paul is coming down the stairs. He looks worried. "Fiona's been sick to her stomach and vomiting for the last two hours. I took her temperature, and it's normal—" but before he's finished, Nora is up the stairs, fast, to Fiona's bedside. Fiona looks miserable. Her face flushed pink, her bangs damp on her forehead.

"Mommy," she cries. "I don't feel so good."

Nora brushes Fiona's bangs to the side and bends down to kiss her cheek, breathing in the faint odors of sweat and vomit.

"It's okay, sweetheart, I'm here now." Nora lies down next to Fiona and gathers her close, pulls the blanket over the two of them, whispers, "Do you know how much I love you?"

Fiona presses hard into Nora, two pieces fitting together like small countries in a private continent. "Beyond the stars and back," Fiona says softly.

"Yes, my love, beyond the stars and back," she says, stroking Fiona's hair until she is asleep.

When Paul comes to the doorway, she whispers, "I think she's fine. Probably just something she ate at school."

He slides a hand slow over his face, through his

hair, says in a voice flat as a granite slab, "I'll be downstairs if you need anything, okay?"

Once he's gone, she thinks about him. The way he's become more and more unstrung—the pressure of his relentless business deals—she's heard him on the phone arguing and dictating terms with bankers and lawyers—the strain of doing more of the housework because she's been too upset to care. Her not wanting to have sex. His obvious affair with Elisa. And she still hasn't said anything to him about Margaret. She can't bring up the right words. *Paul, I might be a multiple personality. Paul, I might be schizophrenic.* She can see his eyes flash alarm, his face stiffen into disbelief, images of his mother tearing through his mind.

No, she isn't ready.

And now, Margaret has called her a liar. An imaginary entity within her, something she's invented in her mind, has called her a *liar*. Fiona whimpers a little, and Nora pulls her closer. She will survive this. She will lean on her logical mind. Logically, something must have happened to hurt her so badly she was unable to face it, is still unable to face it. Has she missed something about her mother's death? Her mother fell down the stairs because she was drunk, not because she, Nora, wouldn't stop playing the piano. Still, she feels guilty, but logically, she knows guilt is a normal response. So, what is she not facing?

Her father's abandonment? Her rational mind knows her father had his own struggles. That he wasn't capable of caring for two children on his own. Yes, it hurts like hell that he completely disappeared, but that couldn't possibly be enough to trigger this—this craziness, this Margaret, this child. Why a child? And why had she prayed to St. Margaret? And why had Margaret called her a liar?

Only one other person in her life had called her a liar.

"Liar!" her mother shouted, snatching the rosary from Nora's six-year-old fist. "Where did you get this?"

"S-s-sister Rosa gave it to me."

"Liar!" Her mother's red hands shaking the rosary close to Nora's face.

"P-p-please Mommy, give it back."

"You want it back? Here!" And then her mother's angry fingers wrenching the rosary apart until SNAP! The white thread breaks, and all fifty-nine blue beads pop into the air and clatter to the floor. Her mother leaving her there then, in the sudden silence of it all, Nora smearing tears off her cheeks and scrambling to find each precious bead.

"Liar!" her mother shrieked the morning she'd found an empty package of lemon-crème cookies in Nora's bed.

"It wasn't me, Mommy," Nora cried. "It wasn't me."

"Liar!" her mother hissed after she'd pulled Nora out of the confessional at church. "You spit on the priest. The priest! Through the screen!"

"But I didn't, Mommy! I didn't!"

She remembers being angry with the priest. But she doesn't remember why or what she'd said. And she doesn't remember spitting on him.

Lying there in the dark, Nora remembers these things. But she doesn't remember why there was an empty package of cookies in her bed. And she does not remember praying to St. Margaret.

CHAPTER FIFTEEN
JANUARY 29, 1997

"I'm worried about Fiona," Nora says to David a couple of days later. She is clutching a paper cup of coffee with both hands. "She's been getting stomachaches. The pediatrician thinks it's anxiety."

"What do you think?" he asks, cleaning his glasses with the bottom of his shirt.

"Well, I think he's probably right." She puts her cup down next to her ankles and rubs her fingers hard into both her temples. "I stayed home with her the last couple of days, and she seemed to feel better quickly. We had such a lovely time, but . . ." she closes her eyes and rubs her temples even harder.

"But it wasn't enough," he says.

"No." She thinks of the last few days with Fiona, how they'd spent almost every moment together, played dress-up, Fiona becoming a princess in an evening gown Nora had found at a garage sale, read *Heidi*, *Little House in the Big Woods*, *Charlotte's Web*. They'd written a funny story about an onion named Miss Pearl, sung along with Patsy Cline's "I Fall to Pieces," Fiona dramatically falling to the ground each time the chorus came around and then breaking into giggles. It had been such a relief to hear her laugh, the sound of it bright as a sunrise, and yet there had been moments, too, when Fiona reached for her and wouldn't let go, whispering, "Mommy, Mommy, Mommy," and Nora had tried not to fall to pieces. You can't keep secrets from children. Fiona knows something is wrong, and her worries are making her sick.

"Nora?"

She opens her eyes, folds her hands on her lap. "Presidents' Day break is coming up next week, and I'm spending every free moment with her. I just wish I could understand what's going on in my head and be done with it without . . . damaging her."

David leans forward, giving her the whole attention of his being. "What you are working through is the opposite of damaging, to you or Fiona. Your healing will be the greatest gift you can give her. Concealing your pain keeps a part of you in darkness, and trust me, *that* isn't good for anyone."

She tells herself he is probably right, she is doing the right thing. In a few months everything will be fine again. She promises herself she will take charge of this; she will resolve it.

"Nora, do you want to talk about our last session? When you left you were pretty upset."

She should tell him about the other times she was called a liar, about the broken rosary, but she

121

is aware now that she is becoming sleepy, and she has the vague awareness these feelings are the ones preceding the appearance of Margaret. This awareness frightens her, and she quickly sits up straight and takes a large gulp of coffee. *She is in charge here.*

"Nora, what were you feeling the night after our last session?"

After Fiona had fallen asleep, after she had remembered the other times she'd been called a liar, she'd crept down to the kitchen and eaten a fistful of cookies, then bread with butter and jam, and then more cookies. And then she'd vomited it all into the toilet. But she doesn't tell David these things—she can't.

"Nora, how do you feel about Margaret calling you a liar?"

Nora tries to speak then, but when she opens her mouth, the silence in the room rushes into every pore of her, until, with the huge weight of it, she closes her eyes and her head falls to her chest.

"Don't look at me," she says, her head down. Her voice a higher pitch.

"Margaret?"

"Please—please, can you sit in the other chair?" Margaret says, and she carefully peeks as David moves to the green chair by the window. He is old and moves slowly, like her grandfather, and she thinks he also looks like him, which makes her feel safer. David turns his head to the window like last time. She can see the black of the night sneaking in through the cracks in the blinds. She needs to tell him. It is her job.

"I'm glad you are here, Margaret."

"Mommy broke our rosary and I tried to find all the beads but I couldn't find them all and it was me who spit in the priest's face," she says. She cannot stop shaking. His hands are wrapped around his coffee mug, and he stays looking at the blinds when he talks. It could be a trick, but she doesn't think so because his body is leaning back.

"And I'm the one who ate the cookies in bed," she says watching him, watching the door. "I ate the cookies because Daddy tasted yucky and I'm really, really sorry." No one is coming in, but she will talk fast. "And I stole money from Daddy's suit pockets and also I steal money from Paul. I keep it in an orange shoe box with the rosary beads in Nora's closet . . . the one with the little white check mark." She stops then and watches him look out the window for a long time without speaking, like he's thinking and will never talk to her again because of all the bad things she has done. She can't think of what else to do right now, but then he talks.

"Margaret, why did you steal money from your daddy?"

"Because . . . because . . . I needed it. I was

saving up for me and Nora to run away." She is really scared now and keeps looking at the door in case someone comes in and she has to get away fast.

"Margaret, can I ask you one more question?"

No one is coming in now, and David is not mad about the money, so she says, "Yes."

"Why did you spit in the priest's face?"

She closes her eyes tightly. She grabs the pillow and brings her legs up to her chest until she is a tight ball, but then she is right there in the smell of incense, and she is kneeling and waiting and waiting and waiting for the red light to turn green on the big box where the priest waits. Now the red light turns green, and it is her turn, and she tiptoes up to the big box, opens the large door, and steps in, heart stammering, kneels with her face close to the little closed window and now the window slides open and there is a black screen and she can see the shadow of the priest's face and hear his breathing.

"Bless me father for I have sinned," she says shyly. It is only her second time in the big box of confession and she does not know this priest because this is not the church where her school is and she doesn't know why her mother came here instead of their regular church.

"And what are your sins my child?" She is scared to tell him the bad things, but her mother says you have to tell *everything* if you don't want to go to hell. She takes a big breath and says "I . . . I did a very, very, very, bad thing."

"You are too little to do a very, very, very bad thing. So tell me. Tell me what you did wrong."

"I . . . I . . . I . . . touched . . ." She can't tell him. This is too scary.

"You touched what, my child? Something your mother asked you not to?"

"I touched . . . I touched . . ."

The priest leans his face close to the screen. "What did you touch? Tell me. Remember, whatever you tell me is a secret between you and me and God. No one else will ever know."

"I . . . I . . . touched . . . daddy's hard thing."

"His . . . hard thing?"

"The . . . the . . . hard thing between his legs. He put my hand down there in his pants and I touched it and he moved my hand up and down and up and down and—"

"Stop!" the priest says. "Stop saying such things. Why would a nice little girl like you make up such bad things? Did your teacher not tell you to honor your father and mother? Why would you tell such lies?"

"Because. I told you. I am a very, very, very bad girl," and she starts to cry.

"I want to know what you did exactly. Tell me."

She whispers the words between her sobs. "Daddy . . . he . . . put my hand on his hard thing

125

and he said you are my little princess, my little princess, my little princess, and he . . . he . . . put my face on his lap and he—" but she stops then because she can hear the priest breathing hard and she knows he must be getting angry about her being such a horrible little girl and he might break through the screen and slap her or tell her mother or—

"He what? Did you put his hard thing in your mouth?" the priest asks, so close to the screen now, his breathing faster, faster, faster. She can feel his breathing now and his voice is strange and suddenly he sounds like Daddy and she is scared so much and knows something is wrong. She stands up and spits at the screen and runs from the box.

"Margaret," David says. "It's okay. It's okay. No one will hurt you. You are safe. I promise. No one will hurt you. It's okay now. You are here. With me. David. You are safe."

"He . . . he sounded like Daddy and I hated him and spit on him and he told our mother and she beat up Nora so hard because I was such a bad, bad, bad girl!"

"Oh, Margaret," he says, "I am so sorry this happened to you. I'm so sorry. You are not a bad girl! You are not!"

"I *AM* a bad girl!" she screams and she bursts up from the tight ball into a frenzy and runs to

126

the door and slams her head against it, SLAM, SLAM, SLAM! And then the monster's hands are grabbing her shoulders and loud horrible sounds are coming from him and she twists around and there he is! She raises her fists and fights him, kicks out at him, pounds her fists into his head but the monster is too strong for her and grabs her wrists and she screams, "Let me go! Let me go!"

"Stop!" shouts David. "Stop! I am not him! I am not him! I am David. I am David!" And his grip on her wrists loosens, and she sees it is not the monster. It *is* David. Her mouth is frozen open, but she stops screaming and stares at him, her face wet with tears, and he drops her wrists and she crumbles to the floor into a ball and hides her face between her shaking knees and rocks and rocks, sobbing in quick, ragged breaths.

"I am not him," David says again, kneeling in front of her.

Margaret looks up at him then, still whimpering, and here is his white hair and the safe room and the green chair and green couch and the pillow with the raven on it.

"Margaret. No one will hurt you now. No one. Ever again." And he holds her hands together within his, like a prayer, and slowly, slowly, slowly she stops rocking and closes her eyes.

David calls for Nora. She opens her eyes and finds she is sitting on the floor, her back against the door in David's office. He is kneeling down in front of her.

"Oh, my God!" she shouts, jumping up. "Oh, my God, what the hell?"

"Nora, please," he says, standing. "It's okay."

"It's okay? What the hell? Why was I on the floor?"

He looks uncertainly at her. "Margaret was here. Please, can you please just sit on the couch?"

She sits. Her heart thudding. She looks to her left and to her right as if to see if *someone* is there. She looks at her watch. It's an hour later than when she looked a few moments ago. She looks at David. "Shit," she whispers.

"It's all right," he says. "It's all right."

She puts her head in her hands. Her forehead hurts.

"Nora, did you hear anything?" he asks.

"No," she says, her teeth chattering. "No, I didn't hear anything." She rocks back and forth, her head still in her hands. She is caught in a nightmare, but it is not a nightmare. It is a cutting reality, an aggressive invasion of her sanity.

And then David is saying things that don't make sense. Things about stolen money and orange shoe boxes and boxes of confession, and she is trying to listen, trying to understand, but it's all too much. Too much. Too many pieces careening through her mind, smashing reason and logic to smithereens.

David walks to the couch and sits by her.

She doesn't move. "There's something else isn't there?" she asks in a barely audible voice.

He hesitates. She can feel him shifting his body to face her more directly. "Nora, I think this might be enough for today."

"Tell me," she says, staring straight ahead.

"Nora," he says, his voice very even, very serious, "she said, 'I am a bad girl.' She said, 'Daddy forced me to touch his penis.' "

His words: a punch in the face.

Nora keeps her eyes straight ahead, but the blow is dizzying, her eyes bleeding red.

"Nora . . ."

"No," she says, standing up, holding her hand up like a stop sign. "My father would never do such a thing," she says in a gasp before she flees.

She runs home. To the toilet. Lifts the lid. Vomits. Sits on the tub. Head between her knees. "No. No. No," she whispers, teeth chattering. This can't be true; surely, she'd remember, she'd remember, she'd remember the skin the wrinkled flesh the bad thing smell, she'd remember, don't think of this don't make Margaret's memories yours, you are not her, you are not her, this is wrong wrong, wrong, wrong, wrong—

And now, Fiona is calling for her, Paul is shouting, "I got takeout Chinese!" and she stands then, scrubs her hands hard, and walks downstairs to eat dinner with her family.

CHAPTER SIXTEEN
JANUARY 30, 1997

Nora distributes copies of Shakespeare's *The Tempest* to her students. She's too tired to say much about it—only that it was his last play, written in 1610, during the Renaissance. It depresses her that on top of everything else, she has to teach this play—so schizophrenic, one minute serious, the next, foolish. She doesn't need schizophrenic right now.

Her first year teaching Honors English, she'd fought to have *The Tempest* switched to *A Midsummer Night's Dream*, but came up against tenured faculty member Dorothy Bowman. Gray hair clipped close to her scalp, Dorothy was an in-your-face activist and never missed an opportunity to show a student how they could fix the broken world. She thought Shakespeare was a significant historical figure implicated in the politics of his time. She believed *The Tempest* was concerned with European domination of New World natives, interpreting Caliban not as a monstrous villain but as a heroic rebel against Prospero's oppression.

"Are you saying it was a *coincidence* that British Colonization was underway at the exact moment the play was written and performed?"

she'd said loud into Nora's face, hazel eyes snapping. She even quoted Caliban, slamming her fist on the table, " 'This island's mine, by Sycorax my mother, which thou tak'st from me.' " And then shaking her head in a condescending way, "Of course, Shakespeare intended to show oppression."

"How can you know what Shakespeare intended?" Nora had said, face flushing. "He's been dead over four hundred years. You can't know. And since when do we advance our own agendas?" Nora knew full well they did it all the time, but still, doing it with art, with literature, really bothered her. "Aren't we supposed to challenge our students to come to their own conclusions? Their own truths?"

"Their own truths?" Dorothy said. "Most of them walk in here laden with patriarchal attitudes. It's our job to enlighten. Period."

And then, first-year faculty member Bruce Baker, a math teacher with a psychology minor, had weighed in. Bruce, who was assigned freshman English at the last minute because Denise Abano quit to start an olive oil business in Pike Place Market—*Too many desperate kids,*" she'd said to Nora over the phone. *"Too many. Coming to school hungry, hopeless, drugged out. Where are the parents? Where are the goddamned parents?"* Bruce, with his new-teacher glow, voted to keep *The Tempest*. "They must love it," he'd said, "a banished dude seeks revenge using magic!" His knowledge surprised Nora, since English wasn't his thing. "My dad's in the theater," he'd shrugged. "Played Prospero seven times." When Nora suggested they switch plays, she'd teach *Romeo and Juliet* and he could have *The Tempest*, he raised a hand, said, "Oh, no, no, no, no. If I have to hear *'We are such stuff as dreams are made on'* and *'How our little life is rounded with sleep'* one more time, I'll fucking kill myself." He'd tapped his pencil on the table then. Looked at her hard. "Yeah, and the whole rape thing, that's gotta be a bitch to explain. I couldn't do it. I mean a father wants to rape his own daughter. That's so fucked up."

"What the hell are you talking about? Prospero didn't rape Miranda," Nora had said, her heart rate increasing, startling her. "Caliban wanted to—"

"Oh, come on," Bruce interrupted, no longer tapping his pencil. "The Freudian paradigm? Caliban *is* Prospero's id. Ariel's his superego. Do the math. Prospero wanted to rape his own daughter."

"Oh, jeez," Nora said in a dismissive way, though a sudden flood of heat into her face had contradicted her nonchalance, flustered her for a moment.

"See, this is what I'm talking about," she said. "Forcing art into some cultural scheme."

She arranged her notes into a neat pile and placed them into a file folder. Tucked a bit of hair behind her ear. Looked at him, looked at Dorothy. "I just want a more relevant story, that's all. *A Midsummer Night's Dream* has the anguish between young people, the impact of inequality on a relationship, and it deals with beauty, or what we call beauty, what beauty really is, not the clichés, something internal. I just want—I just want to offer art and let the art work its magic. Let the art shape them, find them—" but she stopped then, realized she was rambling.

"It's all moot anyway," Dorothy said. "There's no money for new books."

Nora remembers how distraught she'd become in that discussion, especially when Bruce brought up Caliban as a projection of Prospero's desires. She hadn't questioned her feelings then, had merely felt she'd spoken her mind with conviction and passion. But now, with David's suggestion of PTSD, maybe there was more.

She said, "Daddy forced me to touch his penis."

A wave of nausea slams her. She considers running out of the classroom, running the five blocks to the ferry and jumping on board, and on the other side, boarding a bus to Canada and never coming back again. She's on dangerous ground, and she knows it. She clings fast to herself, breathes slow and deep into the sick feeling, deep and slow until she can continue. "It was the age of discovery," she says to the class now, her voice quivery. "A time when Europeans were expanding the geographical horizon of the people of the Middle Ages, when people thought the world only consisted of Europe, Africa, and Asia."

"You mean a time when white bastards took over land that wasn't theirs and called those lands *new* worlds?" Elizabeth says.

"There are those, many in fact, who would agree with you," Nora says, but keeps her opinions to herself, fights the urge to shout, *Yes! White bastards, fucking assholes!* "And others who read it purely as an artistic story without a political bent."

"Well, Shakespeare wasn't an idiot, was he?" Jaleesa says. "So of course this is political."

"Ummm, seems kind of obvious what this is about," Jason says, studying the book's cover, "There's a big-ass storm and a ship and a pissed off god in the sky shooting fire at it and—"

"You mean goddess," Jaleesa says. "Don't you see her long red hair, her flowing gown?" And then, "Though of course, it is a *white* goddess. When are we ever going to read something with a *black* goddess?"

"Well, this goddess is pissed," Lidia says. "Whoever's in that ship is screwed."

"I hope she kills them all," Elizabeth says.

"Well, she'll probably kill all but one guy, and

he'll swim to the island, blah, blah, blah," Jason says. "Typical shipwreck story."

"We don't know which side of colonization Shakespeare was on," Elizabeth says, ignoring them, staring at the cover. "But I'll bet he's against it. He cared about art and beauty. He'd make the mariners survive so they'd know what it feels like to be tormented and controlled by something stronger." Her tone is angry, and she continues to stare at the cover. She sits very still, very straight in her black T-shirt and baggy camouflage pants, her black combat boots. Nora is worried about her. She's been increasingly edgy lately, her body and face so tight. Nora makes a mental note to catch Elizabeth after class, find out what's going on, let her know she's not alone.

"It could be like *Lord of the Flies*," Jason says. "Fear and survival. Attack and murder. Primal. Totally primal."

"Shakespeare's a dick. A sexist pig," Susan says, daughter of doting helicopter parents who make sure she has the best education, Tommy Hilfiger clothing, all the necessary orthodontia. "I mean most of the women in his plays seem like victims. Don't you think he's sexist, Mrs. Brown?"

Nora leans on her desk, shifts her weight. "Well, in the context of the conventions of his day . . ."

"Yeah, it's like, now we know Spam sucks, but

in the fifties it was totally cool," Jason says.

"What about Queen Elizabeth?" Lidia asks. "She ran England when Shakespeare was alive."

"She was an exception," Nora says. "Most women then had a pretty raw deal. And don't think she had it easy. People came up with all kinds of reasons for her success—that she was a man in disguise, for example, or that she surrounded herself with men because she was too stupid to make her own decisions. Only recently has her success been attributed to her brilliance." Nora pauses for a moment. Her eyes meeting all the curious eyes looking at her, listening to her. Tiny surges of strength fire through her body, and she feels a singular awareness of who she is now, in this moment. She *is* a teacher. She *is* strong. She *is not* her past. She continues as if the earlier nausea, the fears, never existed, her voice clear and confident. "Women during Shakespeare's time were a long way from having any rights and were in one way or another the property of men, either their fathers or their husbands." She thinks then of Ophelia and her parting shot, her suicide, her refusing to be the plaything of men. "There's still a huge battle ahead for equality," she says.

"So you're a feminist?" Elizabeth asks.

"Well, yes, of course."

Elizabeth smiles slightly.

Jason says, "My brother says feminists are haters. Feminazis."

"Hmmm," Nora says. "No denying feminism is a loaded word, and when people are threatened, they look for something negative. But it doesn't mean we should run from the word—that would be kind of what the name-callers want, right? Millions of people around the world suffer from racism, sexism, and extremism, and feminists are people who want equal rights for *all* people, regardless of sex or gender, so until those rights are equal, until everyone receives equal pay for the same job, until everyone has equal representation in government, until all people in every country can vote, have rights to their own bodies, yeah, I'm a feminist."

"My mom's pretty happy about Janet Reno getting appointed attorney general," Chrissy says, trying to diffuse things.

"Is Reno a woman?" Jason asks, smirking. "She looks like a man. An ugly man."

"Jason," Nora says. "Considering half the population is female, and less than 16 percent are represented in Congress, Clinton's appointment of Reno was pretty important for feminism. Reno is now one of the most powerful people in the government. And she's also a constant reminder that femininity looks different for every woman—she's changing the standard for beauty."

"Unlike male rappers," Susan says, glaring at Trevor, a tall, black kid drumming his fingers on his desk, making musical instrument sounds with his mouth.

"What you talkin' 'bout?" Trevor says. "I don't put women down."

"Seriously? It's like every other word is 'bitch' and 'ho,' and you're always saying things like 'The girl's been had,' like she's some kind of object."

"Hey, man, I'm just representin' what's around me," Trevor says. "You don't like it, start your own group. Damn, why you get so angry?"

"It's up to all of you to educate yourselves, organize, and take up the unfinished business of the movement for equality," Nora says. "Now, turn to Act I, Scene I, and let's talk about iambic pentameter."

Nora sits at her desk eating tuna out of a plastic container and tries hard to focus on grading papers.

"Mrs. Brown?" Elizabeth leans on the doorframe.

Nora sets her fork in the container and wipes her mouth with a paper napkin. Elizabeth looks formidable with her hard-edged posture and Kurt Cobain T-shirt. If she can stay in school, she's one of those young women who could change the world.

"Hey, Elizabeth. What's up?"

"I was wondering if I could talk to you about this?" She holds out a copy of Toni Morrison's *The Bluest Eye*.

"Yes, of course. Have a seat."

Elizabeth sits, straight up, her face tight. She clutches the book to her breast.

"Elizabeth, are you okay?"

"My mother's forming a committee to ban this from the school library. God, she's so ignorant, so inane."

Nora stands and walks around to the front of her desk, leans against it. "Did she say why?"

"Pornography. Can you believe it? Where is there pornography in this book?"

Nora shakes her head. "That's wrong. So wrong." A slight thudding begins in her chest.

"I love this book," Elizabeth says. "I love the little girl, Pecola." She holds the book again to her breast, and her eyes well. "It makes me so sad to think of her praying for blue eyes—that she thought everything would be all right if only she had blue eyes—that if she had them, someone would love her and her life would be saved and things would be different." And now, Elizabeth is crying, tears spilling down her cheeks.

Nora reaches for a box of Kleenex from her desk, holds it out to her. This girl breaks her heart. This girl knows something about anger and pain and sadness. Nora wants to pull her close, take her home, and wrap her in a fluffy blanket.

Elizabeth pulls out a Kleenex, wipes her eyes. "And you know what's really fucked up?"

"What?" Nora says quietly.

"That she thought if she had blue eyes *she* would see differently." Her words break apart.

"That it's not—it's not the rest of us who are messed up—it's *her*."

"She was a victim," Nora says in a soft voice. "She didn't get to have a normal teenage life, if there is such a thing. She didn't get to discover life, let alone her sexuality, on her own terms." Heat rises in her chest. "Makes me angry," she whispers. "Men and their power issues."

Elizabeth looks at her then, just looks at her and stays quiet for a while—and then her face softens, and she says through her tears, "You know what's really wrong? That the narrator makes it seem like if her father hadn't been humiliated as a child he might not have hurt Pecola. Like *he's* a victim or something! It was his fault! It's the entire town's fault!" She catches her breath and then whispers, "And now if the book is banned, it's like we're silencing her all over again."

Nora leans over and puts her arms around her. "I'll fight for the book, Elizabeth. I promise."

That night Nora awakens from a recurring bad dream—the one where she runs through a dangerous neighborhood at night looking for her car. She runs past junkies and barred windows and pimps who shout things at her: *"Hey baby, come to Daddy."* And then, ahead, her car, and shit! There are punks vandalizing it, and she hides—always in the same place, between two old brick buildings—and watches, heart thudding, as the punks rip apart her VW Bug. She watches, cramped and panicked, her hand over her mouth as they wrench off the tires, smash the windows, and tear out the stereo. The one in the black ski mask flips out a blade and gouges a jagged line from the driver's door to the rear bumper before they all run, arms carrying things that belong to her, into the darkness. Nora scans the street, and when she's sure they're gone, she makes herself walk to the stripped car. She stands near the heap of red metal, sickened by the trespass, her entire body trembling in the silence and confusion.

"God, that's so *classic*," Paul had said to her, years ago, when she'd described the nightmare. "A classic dream of stolen identity. You don't know who you are."

His remarks had infuriated her at the time, though she'd finally dismissed them, believing he'd been frustrated because they hadn't had sex in months, but now thoughts of Margaret, her words, *I am a bad girl,* infiltrate her mind, nausea rising into her throat until she can no longer stay in bed but must go to the closet in search of the orange shoe box. She can't go on feeling the way she does, inhabited by an imaginary being making outrageous claims. She will prove Margaret isn't real, prove she's purely a symptom of fatigue, frantic hormones, or an iron deficiency or something.

Nora slips into the closet like an unarmed thief.

She shuts herself inside and turns on the light. It's a huge closet. On the left: Paul's shirts (at least twenty white and blue Ralph Lauren oxfords), sport jackets, and pants (ten pleated khaki, ten black dressy, a half a dozen jeans) hang neatly, and underneath it all, ten pairs of black dress shoes and ten pairs of athletic shoes planted precisely on a metal shoe tree. On the right: her mess. Blouses, skirts, dresses, and coats—a palette of blues, blacks, and grays hang sloppily in no particular order, some piled on the floor, mixing in with her dirty clothes until she can't tell the difference.

There's a safe feeling here though, one of containment and familiarity. When she was little she'd spent hours and hours alone in her closet, hiding there with her flashlight to read and write stories about trees and birds and worlds that made sense. Sometimes, after her mother had too many gins, James would find her and ask with a look that alarmed her if he could come in too. And then later he'd say, tearfully, "Let's never go out."

Now, she pushes to the back of the closet, where she keeps the shoes she doesn't wear but might someday, and notices, as if for the first time, the number of shoe boxes, at least thirty, stacked high and in no apparent order. *Saucony, Brooks, New Balance, Birkenstock, Doc Martens, Steve Madden, Nine West, Vera Wang.* There is only one Vera Wang pair. She'd found the glittery, flirty shoes at a consignment store years ago and had hoped to wear them to a Clinton Inaugural event at the Seattle Center, but when Paul said there was no way in hell he'd go with her, no way he'd ever support a fucking "New Democrat," she'd decided not to go after all but kept the shoes anyway.

Her eyes scan the columns for the orange box with the white check mark—a Nike box. She would be surprised if she still had Nikes, was sure she'd thrown out the few she had when she'd heard the allegations of abuse in their factories in Asia, their exploitation of children as laborers. But there it is, an orange Nike box, near the bottom of the first column of boxes.

She stares at it, her heart racing like a caged animal. She grits her teeth, refusing to let herself panic, and stretches her body up to remove the boxes above the orange one so the entire column doesn't fall. By the time she finally gets to the Nike box, her hands are shaking. She hesitates for a moment, then picks it up. It is heavy, and immediately there is the jangle of coins. She sets the box on the floor, kneels, and with trembling hands removes the lid. It's full of pennies, nickels, dimes, and quarters. She touches the coins as if they might not be real. Then she notices things under the coins. A small brown box, a tiny white envelope, and folded pieces of notebook paper. She opens the brown box first. Draws a breath.

Her rosary beads—the beads from the rosary her mother had broken. Her cheeks blazing, remembering that moment, Nora counts the opaque blue beads. Forty-nine. She remembers ten beads had been lost. And here is the crucifix. She remembers placing the forty-nine beads with the crucifix in a jar under her bed, and once her mother had died, once she'd been sent to Ireland, she'd never seen the beads again. *How is this possible?* Could she really have forgotten she'd found them? Placed them in this box in her closet?

She picks up the white envelope. No writing on either side. She opens it. A holy card. A pin-pricking charge ripples across her skin. On the front, a woman with a ring of stars around her head, body draped in purple, a gold sword held high, her right foot on a dragon's head. On the back, typed words in gilded print: ST. MARGARET, PATRON SAINT OF THE FALSELY ACCUSED AND THOSE IN EXILE, HELP US. Nora sits perfectly still in the silence. Eyes fixed on the holy card, the beads, the coins, items she has no recollection of saving in this box. A realization hits her hard—she needs to take Margaret very seriously. Margaret may be an invention of her consciousness, ludicrous, contrary to reason, but nonetheless, Margaret knows things. Things that Nora does not. *Still,* Nora thinks, nausea rising again, *that doesn't mean her words about my father are true.* "Go away," Nora whispers out loud to Margaret. *"Please go away."*

And finally, the white notebook paper. She unfolds the pages slowly. It's a story she'd written on her tenth birthday. She remembers writing this. She'd gone into her closet one afternoon to stay out of her mother's way until her father got home. He was going to bring a birthday cake.

Promises

Once, a long time ago, a mother and father took their new baby girl across the sea to Ireland to have it baptized by an Irish priest because the mother said Irish priests were closer to God than priests in Chicago and because the mother had not seen her family since she was eighteen years old and now she is twenty-one. In America she met her husband and married him.

On the morning of the baptism, it was very stormy and the hawthorn trees outside the church were shivering in the wind and people had to bend their heads down just to walk. The grandmother and grandfather and seven aunts and their husbands and two uncles and their wives and one uncle who was too young to have a wife yet and twelve children were going to the baptism. The neighbors were going too. Everyone walked for miles in a long line to the church.

The father looked extremely handsome, like a prince. He was twenty-two years old. He wore a navy-blue suit with a white shirt and a sea-green tie. He wanted to wear his new black hat but it kept blowing off in the wind so he carried it in his hand. The mother wore a lovely violet dress and a matching violet hat pinned into her long, flaming-red hair.

The baby wore a special white gown worn by her mother at her own baptism. The gown was made by the mother's great-great-grandmother Brighid. She knit the white gown from the finest white yarn. She made the yarn herself from the wool of her own fine sheep.

Babies must wear white to show they are spotless in the eyes of God.

Everyone went inside the church except for the grandfather who waited outside because he didn't like churches.

Inside the church, it was dark, it was very dark and the baby became scared and began to cry and so the mother carried her to a life-size statue of the Virgin Mary up by the altar. The Virgin Mary held out her arms out as if she wanted to hold the baby. The baby stared at the statue and stopped crying.

The mother stood with the father and the

priest in front of everyone and held the baby tight in her arms. An altar boy dressed in white held a golden tray with two golden chalices upon it. One chalice was filled with holy water and the other held perfumed oil blessed by the bishop. The water would wash away the sins of the baby and give her new life. The oil would give the baby power from the Holy Ghost.

The priest sprinkled drops of holy water and perfumed oil on the baby's forehead and said to the father in a loud voice, "Do you promise to love this baby with all your heart and soul?"

And the father said, "Yes, I promise."

And the priest said, "Do you promise to protect her from all harm?"

And the father said, "Yes, I do."

And then the priest said to the mother, "Do you promise to love this baby with all your heart and soul?"

And the mother said, "Yes, I promise."

And the priest said, "Do you promise to protect her and keep her safe and protect her from all harm?"

And the mother said, "Yes, I promise."

And then the priest turned to the Godparents and asked them to make promises too.

Then the priest took the baby from the

mother and lifted her up high and said, "I baptize thee Nora in the name of the Father and the Son and the Holy Spirit. Oh, Almighty God, may you bless this child and help her mother and father keep their promises forever and if they don't, please help save the girl. Amen." And then all the people in the church said, "Amen," and the priest gave the baby back to the mother.

After the baptism everyone walked down the road to the pub to celebrate because the baby's soul was saved. When they got there the mother was tired and she set the baby on a hard bench and went to get a drink at the bar. The baby became frightened and started to cry but the grandfather came and held her in his arms. He dipped his finger in whiskey and put it on her lips and sang, "The violets were scenting the woods, Nora, displaying their charm to the bee," until the baby fell asleep.

Nora wipes her eyes and wills her hands to place everything back in the box, wills them to put the lid on and shove it back into place, piling the other boxes, one by one, on top of it. She will not think about this anymore tonight.

CHAPTER SEVENTEEN
JANUARY 31, 1997

The next morning, Nora sits at her desk sipping coffee and writing comments on essays. It is necessary she keep her head in the game and not dwell on confessionals, shoe boxes, and saints. Outside the door, students slam lockers, establishing their positions by calling each other names: Gay. Loser. Shithead. The word "fuck" replacing most of their verbs, some of their nouns, and all of their adjectives. She takes a deep breath and opens the door. "Good morning," she says, pretending cheerfulness to each one as they drift in, morose and heavy-lidded.

Once they are seated and she's taken attendance, she stands in front of her desk, leans on it, smiling and fighting an urge to run from the room.

"Okay," she says, "today we'll begin with a freewrite."

There are a few groans from the audience but mostly grins. Freewrites are easy for most of them—they like that there's no right or wrong. "Remember," she says, "this isn't about sounding smart or clever. It's about listening to your thoughts and recording them in whatever way they come out." She feels then, suddenly, that someone is behind her, though she knows there isn't, how could there be? No one has left their seat or come in the door. She resists the urge to look over her shoulder, but still, the pervasive sensation unnerves her.

"I hate freewrites," Jessica mutters, slumping back in her seat and sucking on a strand of her hair.

Good, Nora thinks. *Good. Focus your attention on her. The girl who likes math because there are answers. Look at her. You are the teacher.* Nora moves to the whiteboard and picks up an orange Magic Marker. *Orange. The orange box. Shit. Don't go there. You are the teacher. Teach.* Nora plucks the cap off the marker and draws the outline of a brain with a wiggly line splitting it in two. It looks like a cracked lima bean. She does this sometimes, teaches them how the brain works. She points to the drawing and says with a forced steadiness, "Jessica, here's the thing. When you freewrite, you know, just free associate and write as if no one will read it, you're tapping into the right side of the brain." Nora taps the right side of her drawing with the Magic Marker, surprised she can act as if she's fine. "The right side can offer us discoveries," she continues, "aha moments, ideas no one ever thought of before. I mean, don't get me wrong, important things happen over here, too"—she taps the left side of her drawing—"but"—now she points to the right side, draws a light bulb with an exclamation point inside it—"here in the right hemisphere—well, this is where the *new stuff* happens. And honestly, Jessica, if you want to come up with some new mathematical equations someday, you might want to spend some time over here."

Jessica considers Nora for a moment, smirks, and says, "Whatever," but picks up her mechanical pencil as if she may indeed write.

"Okay, everyone, go ahead and begin," Nora says and begins to walk up and down the aisles, watching pencils slide over paper, thoughts like freed prisoners finally breathing fresh air.

Except for Elizabeth, who sits there with her notebook closed.

"Elizabeth?"

"I have nothing to write about," Elizabeth says, not looking up, tapping on her notebook with the eraser-end of her pencil.

Nora bends down and rests her elbows on Elizabeth's desk. She'd tried to talk to her after the *Bluest Eye* conversation, but Elizabeth had only looked at her shoes and mumbled, "I'm fine." And when Nora had pressed her, said, "Are you sure?" Elizabeth had looked at her for a moment, eyes full of tears, but then turned away and walked down the hall.

"Elizabeth, what's going on?"

"I don't know what to write."

"Well, maybe start with 'I don't remember'? That prompt gets me started sometimes when I'm stuck."

"What's the meeting after school about?" Elizabeth whispers.

Nora has a meeting at 3:00 with Elizabeth and her parents, some of her teachers, and the school counselor to discuss Elizabeth's lack of progress in her classes.

"Is it about *The Bluest Eye*?"

"No, that meeting is in a few weeks. Today is—well, your parents are concerned about you," Nora says. Elizabeth's eyes are so tired, so glazed with sleeplessness. "It'll be okay. Really."

"Fuck my parents."

"Elizabeth, listen. We can't talk about this right now. Okay? We'll talk after school."

Elizabeth jerks her notebook open and begins to write, pressing hard into her paper.

Nora stands up and leaves her. She feels guilty. Twice in the last month, Nora watched Elizabeth rip her freewrites from her notebook, ball them up, and throw them in the wastebasket. And both times, after class, Nora unfolded them and read them. She'd read the pages of ugliness, horrible sentences of self-loathing, lines and loops plunging deep into bottomless holes, and when she'd tried to talk with Elizabeth (not confessing she'd read the notes, how could she?), said, "If you ever need anything, please ask," but of course Elizabeth didn't ask, so Nora had felt obligated to show the notes to Joyce Robertson, the school counselor, and now there's a meeting.

Nora walks by Joe. He's wearing headphones and a stained T-shirt that says EXCUSE ME FOR STARING. He is drawing some sort of multiheaded creature on a tree with dead branches. He glances up at Nora with a smirk that is slightly defiant.

"Cool," Nora says, admiring his drawing. And she means it. He is a talented artist, his attention to detail, exquisite. "I sure wouldn't mind being able to see from every direction," she says.

His smirk morphs into a smile, and he keeps drawing. She's not going to require more of him in this moment. She knows what he's up against, living alone with his older brother who's the night manager at 7-11. Once, after Joe had yelled at his math teacher, "I don't have time for fucking homework, you fucking moron," the school counselor told the faculty that Joe did all the cooking and cleaning at his house and to please try and cut him some slack.

Nora walks to her desk and sits down—her head beginning to throb. She allows the students to write until the end of the period. She pretends to grade essays. Neurons firing glass shards into the vessels of her brain.

On her way to the meeting, things are magnified. Students just released from classrooms pour into the hallway, sweaty, in various moods

153

and behaving with conspicuous nuances. Mouths open and close, and sounds come at her in scratching flats and sharps. Arms wave loosely. Lockers slam. Slam over and over again, the deafening slam slam slam and she wants to clap her hands to her ears, but of course she doesn't. She rushes in and out through bodies, arms, and huge faces breathing close from all angles and she moves in and out, and shit, this must be how a bad acid trip feels, and she rushes into the faculty bathroom, into a stall, locks the door, mind raw, eyes blinking fast.

She is safe.

She sits on the toilet. Listens. A toilet flushes. A door opens. Clicking of heels. A faucet shoots water. Paper towel ripped, crumpled. Clicking of heels. A door opens and shuts with a thud. The clicking heels echo down the hall. Silence.

She shudders. Then, thoughts of Elizabeth. "Damn it," she says half aloud. "Damn it," she says again to something she has no name for. "You will not win." She stands and opens the door.

She is only five minutes late. The counselor, the math teacher, the science teacher, Elizabeth's parents, Elizabeth, and John sit around the large table. Only John and Elizabeth's mother look at her. John smiles at her, and she relaxes a bit.

Nora takes a seat next to him. Rubs her temples. He leans over and whispers, "Really glad you're here." There's a pitcher of water and paper cups in the center of the table, and she leans in to pour herself a cup and drinks it all down. The counselor and the teachers shuffle papers and make small talk. At the other end of the table, Mr. Guenther, Elizabeth's father, sits. He is well-dressed in a suit and tie, thinning black hair slicked back. His clammy face makes Nora look away from him to the mother, who smiles uncertainly at her, her face the same pale white as her daughter's. Elizabeth sits hunched between her parents, looking at her hands on her lap, eyelashes fluttering like trapped moths.

After the counselor, Joyce, makes introductions, she turns to Elizabeth and says, "Elizabeth, we are here today because we're concerned about you. Concerned because you aren't doing your homework, because you are lethargic in class, and, well, because frankly, you aren't really participating *anywhere.*"

Elizabeth continues to look at her hands. Her body becoming smaller, more rigid by the second. Nora wants to go to her and carry her away.

"Elizabeth," her father says. "Do you have anything to say to that?"

Elizabeth shrugs.

"How do you feel about school, dear?" Joyce asks. Her tone is syrupy and limp. She is the type of person who brings a big fruit bowl for the faculty room each Monday and drops off little

155

foil-wrapped muffins in staff mailboxes with tags that say, *"Have a good day! You're making a difference!"*

"I hate it," Elizabeth whispers.

"Elizabeth," her father says, "please speak up, and look at us when we speak to you."

She looks up. Looks only at Nora. Her agitated eyes pierce Nora's heart, but Nora smiles at her reassuringly.

"I want to live full time with Mom," Elizabeth says suddenly, her eyes never leaving Nora's.

The room is silent.

"What?" says Mr. Guenther, inflamed. "What the hell are you talking about? How can you say that?"

"Well, Bill," Mrs. Guenther says, sitting up a little straighter, clearing her throat, "it *is* difficult for her to keep going back and forth. You know, keeping track of everything. Perhaps—"

"Perhaps nothing!" Mr. Guenther says, marching over his wife's words like a tiger tramping on violets. He turns to his daughter. "You will NOT live with your mother full time! If anything, your mother is a huge part of the problem. Are there even any rules at her house? Do you *ever* do your homework over there? Ever?"

"Dad," Elizabeth whispers, looking down. "Please. It would be easier, that's all."

"Easier? Easier?" He is becoming louder.

"Isn't that the whole problem? That you want everything easier? Do you even know what hard work is? Do you?"

When Elizabeth says nothing, he shouts at her, "Look at me, damn it!"

"Mr. Guenther, please," Joyce whines nervously and looks at John to do something.

"Bill," John says, clenching his pen tightly. "Let's calm down here. Our goal here is to help Elizabeth. Losing tempers won't help anyone."

Nora wants to reach over and unfold his fist and leave her hand in his. But she keeps her hands folded together and her eyes on Elizabeth.

Elizabeth looks at Nora then, and her eyes fill with tears. This girl is not the rebel who talks tough in class and smokes behind the school. Nora thinks about the poems, all the stories she's read of Elizabeth's. The freewrites thrown in the garbage. And suddenly, she knows the reason for Elizabeth's self-loathing. She knows. Fury begins to burn inside her, fury at the people around this table, fury at this man, this pathetic fuck of a father. How she wants to lunge at him, wave Elizabeth's writing in his face, scream, "You fucking asshole!" But she is frozen there, torn between betraying Elizabeth and getting her the hell away from this man.

"Fine," her father says with feigned calmness. "If she doesn't do her homework, there should be consequences, that's all. Obviously her mother just lets her run wild, and you people have no idea how to get her to complete her work. If anything, Elizabeth should live with me full time."

Elizabeth looks up then, with such shock on her face, such despair in her eyes, pinpricks of adrenaline shoot through Nora's body, and when Elizabeth whispers, "NO, NO, NO," and the shrunken mother sits there, tight-lipped, doing nothing, and the father says, "No?" and becomes more red-faced, more belligerent and says, "We're done here! I'm taking her out of this wasteland, this pitiful excuse of a school, this"—it is then Nora stands up and goes to Elizabeth, kneels down, and wraps her arms around her.

"Move away from her!" Elizabeth's father says. He stands up, toppling his chair. "I said . . ." He glowers at Nora, everything about him clenched.

"Mr. Guenther!" shouts John, already next to Nora and Elizabeth. "Please. Sit down."

"Elizabeth isn't going anywhere," Nora says evenly. She keeps her arms around Elizabeth. "You will not—" but before she can finish, Elizabeth's father grabs Nora's wrist and jerks her up from her knees.

"Daddy, stop!" Elizabeth cries, jumping up, pushing her father back.

John is already there, pulling him from behind. "Mr. Guenther, enough!" he shouts. "Stop this second or I'll call security!"

Nora wrenches her hand from Mr. Guenther's

and backs away, keeps her eyes on him, the ugly impotence of his being nauseating her.

"Get your things, Elizabeth," he says quietly.

Nora's heart beats violently, the fury within her burning out of control. She pushes between Elizabeth and Mr. Guenther. She looks him in the eyes. She cannot stop herself. "You asshole. You fucking asshole," she says, and punches him in the stomach. She hears him gasp and then his hand is flying hard across her face and now people are shouting and someone is lifting her off the floor—carrying her out of the room, laying her down somewhere soft.

"Are you okay?" It's John. He's pulled up a chair next to her. Brown eyes stunned, worried, nervous. He has an ice pack, and holds it lightly to her cheek.

She winces, resurfaces. Lies motionless for a moment. She is in the faculty room on a couch. She sits up abruptly; the ice pack flies out of John's hand.

"Elizabeth! Where's Elizabeth?" she asks, panicked.

"I'm not sure," John says, his voice stressed. He reaches down and picks up the ice pack from the floor, sets it on the end table. "I was too busy getting you off Mr. Guenther. God, Nora, what the hell happened? You're lucky you weren't hurt any worse."

"We can't let Elizabeth go with him. He's molesting her, John. We have to find her."

John drew a deep breath, then released it as he said, "Nora, do you have evidence? Because if you believe he's molesting her, shit." He stood up, began pacing. "If we're going to help her, we have to think this through. Call CPS before he hurts her again. We have to think through this *carefully*. We don't want to make things any worse for her."

Something hard and hot seethes in Nora again. She doesn't have any evidence. It's all in Elizabeth's notebooks—if it exists anymore at all. "I need to talk to her. Now," Nora says, and stands. "Don't you understand? She's already abandoned herself. I can't abandon her. I won't. I can't. I need to find her." But as she moves to leave, John reaches for her hand, holds it gently.

"Nora. Please. Ok. Let me figure something out. But Nora—we need to talk about what happened in there—at the meeting. We need to talk about what's happening right now." His voice is thick with emotion but he continues. "Nora, over the years, you and I have seen lots of kids like Elizabeth. We've helped them, or at least most of them. We've tried. We've had condescending asshole parents in that conference room, and you've worked through it with them. You made a difference by being rational and firm. You've never raised your voice. Even when you were outraged. Let alone raised your fist. But Nora, you punched a parent today. God knows he deserved it, but still. And right now—this is more than what's going on with Elizabeth. What is it? Please. Can you tell me?" Her hand falls from his like a leaf.

She is quiet. She is bone tired. "Yes," she says. She sits back down on the couch.

He closes the door, sits next to her, puts his jacket around her like a shawl. She looks out the window into the courtyard filled with rhododendrons and ferns and begins to tell him everything—about Margaret, the dissociation, Paul and Elisa, her worries about Fiona. He holds both her hands while she speaks. He wipes her eyes when she weeps. He promises to do everything possible to keep Elizabeth safe. Promises to call Child Protective Services right away. Promises to be there for her whenever she needs him. He tells her she is the bravest person he's ever met.

CHAPTER EIGHTEEN
THE EVENING OF FEBRUARY 1, 1997

Fiona has emptied a box of candy hearts onto her pillow and is sorting them by color. She's wearing her bluebird nightgown and the Minnie Mouse slippers Paul bought for her on their family vacation to Disneyland last year. Innocence surrounds her, makes her appear fragile and ethereal, and Nora feels then a fierce love for her, a need to take her somewhere unceasingly gentle and good, a place without pounding fists and ugly sounds, a place where she can protect her from anyone who might creep fear into her tiny heart. "Did I ever tell you that you are the most wonderful little girl in the universe?" Nora says.

Fiona giggles. "Yes, Mommy, a billion times. But, Mommy! Listen! I need more of these!" she says, holding high a purple candy heart that says HUG ME. "Valentine's Day is soon, and I want to put a heart inside each of the cards I give out."

"Where did you get these?"

Fiona stops counting and looks nervously at Nora. "Elisa gave them to me. She walked with Daddy and me to school this morning, and she gave each of us a box—is that okay, Mommy? Daddy . . . Daddy told me not to tell and I . . . I . . ."

Be calm, be calm, be calm. "Of course that's

okay, honey; she's our neighbor, and she seems very nice."

But of course it doesn't feel okay. It's demoralizing. She'd sensed from the start there was something more between Paul and Elisa then a platonic friendship. But she can't think about that right now, not on top of the day's events.

"Fiona, could you put those away now and get ready for bed?"

"Okay, Mommy, but we can get more, right?"

"Yes, honey, we'll get more. We have two weeks until Valentine's Day. Now clean up." And they *will* have plenty of time. John has placed her on a three-month leave. He had to, she knows that. She is, in fact, grateful and relieved.

Fiona puts the hearts back into the box, one by one, reading each one as she does. Nora wishes only to lie down. Close her eyes. But now, "Mommy, here's one for you! It says, 'Kiss me!' "

Nora looks at Fiona's innocent face, at the pink candy heart in her small hand, at the words KISS ME, and at once something is wrong—nausea rises in her throat. She cups her hand over her mouth, jumps up, runs to the bathroom, and vomits.

"Mommy?"

Nora flushes the toilet, grabs a towel from the rack, sits on the edge of the tub, and wipes her face. Fiona stands in the doorway looking as if she might cry.

"Mommy, are you okay?"

"Yes, yes, of course I am honey," she says, struggling to talk. "I think I just ate something bad for lunch, that's all. I'll be all right. Now could you brush your teeth please, and I'll be right there to tuck you in."

The phone rings. She walks to the bedroom to answer it. It's John.

"Nora—God. I'm so sorry to tell you this," he says.

She already knows. "Elizabeth?" she says faintly, sits down soft on the bed.

"Two hours ago. Cut her wrists," he says, his voice choking up. "No note." The suffering large in his throat.

The phone cold in her hand. *No, Elizabeth. Not this.* She closes her eyes. *Of course there wouldn't be a note. Elizabeth had already left plenty of fucking notes.*

"Fuck," she says into the phone. John says something, but she can't hear him through the aching.

"Mommy, are you coming?" shouts Fiona. Nora whispers goodbye to John and hangs up the phone and stands up slowly, walks slowly to Fiona's room. Fiona is still playing with the candy hearts.

"Mommy," Fiona giggles, jumping up and down on her bed, pushing a candy heart into Nora's face, "you still haven't done what the heart says!" And she begins to chant loudly in a singsong voice, "Kiss me! Kiss me! Kiss me!"

Something ugly and huge pushes and thrashes inside Nora's head and fury forces its way out and the enormous hand of it slaps the heart from Fiona's tiny hand and the heart flies across the room, hits the closet, and drops to the floor. The fury can see that the heart is still alive—the KISS ME gapes mockingly. The fury leaps at it. Dares it to continue gaping, but the KISS ME doesn't stop and the abominable feet of the fury pounds the cursed heart to pieces, again and again and again, using all its strength to kill it, to smash it to dust, to death, to silence. Such strength, but there! The fury has done it. The fury has won.

Dead silence now.

A soft whimper from the bed.

Nora blinks, blinks, blinks. Heart thudding. *Oh, God. Oh, God. Oh, God.* Something's happened. Pink dust by her feet. *What the hell happened?* She remembers the fury rising, but nothing more. *Margaret? Oh, God.*

Nora turns to see Fiona on the bed, stuffing all the candy hearts back into the box as fast as she can, tears streaming down her face.

"Oh, Fiona."

Fiona shoves the box of hearts into her night-stand drawer, climbs back into bed, and pulls the covers over herself so that not even her head shows. Muffled sobs build up and spill out, pool in a pink liquid around Nora's feet.

Nora feels small and evil. The lump of her daughter hiding under the blanket cuts her deep.

"Oh, Fiona," she says softly and climbs into the bed, uncovering her and taking her in her arms. "I'm so sorry, sweetheart, I'm so sorry." Fiona pushes herself into Nora then, thumb in her mouth, sucking hard, cradled in Nora's arms until she falls, finally, asleep.

Nora arrives at the bottom of the stairs just as Paul comes in the door, alcohol on his breath. She'd heard his keys fighting the lock.

"Whoa. You don't look so good," he says.

"Damn you," she whispers and walks into the kitchen.

Paul shrugs off his coat, hangs it in the closet. "Hey, sorry I'm late. But you got my message, right? That work was a barn burner?"

"Really?" she says, with an exhausted edge, pouring herself a glass of red wine. She sits at the table and stares at the glass. Paul pours himself a glass of Jameson and sits across from her.

"What's wrong?" he says.

She sips in silence for a moment. "You weren't working late," she says looking at him, tapping her index fingernail unconsciously on the thin stem of her glass. "You weren't working late," she says again, even though she should have said, "Something horrible happened when you were gone." She keeps on tap-tap-tap-tap-tap-tap-tap-

166

tap-tap-tapping until he speaks and then she stops tapping.

"What are you talking about?"

"You were with Elisa." She needs to be careful now. She begins tapping again. Stares at Paul. She taps for a minute or two. His eyes, weighted with guilt, light fires inside her. "You're fucking her," she says.

His face reddens. He drains his glass, gets up from the table, and goes to the cupboard. He takes the Jameson down again and pours himself another glass. "And what if I am?" he says, finally. "What the hell do you care? We haven't had sex in months! Do you realize that? Do you? And even then, it was like fucking a corpse. You go all rigid the second I put my hands on you." He rakes his fingers through his hair, paces around the kitchen. "Jesus, this is not what a marriage is supposed to be like. I want more than this, Nora."

She blinks through swimming eyes at the raised lettering on her glass: THE KALALOCH LODGE. Paul had stolen this glass at Thanksgiving, smuggled it from the dining room under his tweed jacket, given it to her as memory of the weekend. He's right. She shouldn't care he's fucking Elisa. He deserves better than this. "I'm going to bed," she says, standing up, wiping her eyes.

"Admit it!" he says, flinging the words like stones. "You hate sex! You dress like a boy!

You always have! You're so thin you look like a boy! And since all your 'therapy' "—he makes quotation marks with his fingers around the word "therapy"—"it's . . . it's like you're not even here! You're a zombie! Shit, Nora, what do you expect me to do? Be a monk for the rest of my life?"

She's silent for a long time, then turns from him and walks heavily up the stairs to the bathroom. She closes the door and locks it securely behind her.

She removes her clothes, slowly, her body trembling. She doesn't remember the last time she'd looked at herself without clothes. Now completely naked, her breathing shallow, in the mirror: her body, the straight and narrow of it, hardly there hips and flat, not-quite breasts looking blank, transparent as clear glass. If not for the curls of blonde hair between her stick legs, a boy's body.

There is a knock at the door. She wraps herself in a towel, opens it, tears welling up in her eyes. She will apologize. Ask for help.

"Nora," he says, his mouth tight as a leather strap, "I'm, I'm—" and when she thinks he is going to apologize, say she doesn't look like a boy, he says, "I'm going out."

Once he's gone, Nora walks to the bedroom and covers her naked body with a flannel nightgown. In bed, she tries not to think about Elizabeth and

Paul and the things he said and how she hates her body, hates sex and always has. And now, in her mind, here is Elizabeth, *Oh, God, no, Elizabeth. God, I'm so sorry.* And now, her mind is in high school, down in Bobby Baker's basement and everyone is touching and rubbing and Bobby is touching her, his clammy hands under her sweater grabbing her breasts and she lets him and she feels nothing. And now here is another boy tearing off her Levi's and fucking her, saying fucking her is like fucking a corpse and her wishing she'd die. And how for years after that, until Paul, she'd kept her distance from men. And now, Paul is fucking Elisa. And Elizabeth is dead. She reaches in her nightstand drawer for a sleeping pill. She swallows it and floats away.

CHAPTER NINETEEN
FEBRUARY 2, 1997

Nora rolls over in bed, looks at the alarm clock. 7:00 a.m., which means 9:00 a.m. in Chicago. James will be awake. She needs to hear her brother's voice.

"You did what?" he says when she tells him about the school meeting, how she'd punched a parent in the stomach. Usually, she can tell him most anything, but today she can't bring herself to tell him more than this. She cannot tell him about the hallucinations and the heart of dust (she's ashamed) and the fights with Paul and that she suspects he's having an affair. James doesn't like Paul and will only tell her to leave him and he'll get all wired up and right now she only has the energy to tell him one other thing.

"James, a student of mine—Elizabeth—do you remember her? I've talked about her?"

"Vaguely."

"She died. She's dead."

"God."

"She's fifteen and she killed herself."

"Nora."

"And I knew, I knew her father was molesting her, I knew it, and . . . and . . . I didn't do anything. I didn't do anything,I —"

"Nora—"

She whispers into the phone, "James, I miss you. Will you come here? Can you come here?"

"Nora. I've got something to tell you." His voice choked with feeling. "You might not want me to come after I tell you."

"James, what?"

Silence.

"I've . . . I've seen dad. He's . . . he's in a nursing home in Rochester."

Silence.

An exploding within her. The fury rises up, huge and violent until there is hardly space to breathe and all she can think about is crashing through the bedroom window and killing the beast once and for all, cutting it to pieces, every artery, every vein, the rotten meat dripping and smelling of blood, but now David's voice in her mind, "You're in charge. You're in charge." She won't let the fury take over. She won't, she won't, she won't, she won't.

"Nora, are you there? Talk to me!"

She hangs up the phone and grabs the railings of her headboard. She is in charge. "Stop!" she yells. "Stop!" And to her shock, the fury abates slightly, the throbbing dulling ever so slightly, though it is still there, coiled, ready to spring. The alarm clock rings. Brrrring! Brrrrring! Brrrring! *Oh, God. School. Time to get Fiona to school.*

She watches herself then, watches herself stand

up, so calm and cool, watches herself dress, watches herself wake Fiona, dress and feed Fiona, and when the phone rings and she hears James pleading on the machine, *"Nora, please call me back,"* she watches herself wink at her daughter, hears herself tell Fiona she'll call James back later, that now it's time to walk to school.

CHAPTER TWENTY
FEBRUARY 2, 1997

The walk to school with Fiona grounds her a bit—the cold air with its salty bite fusing with traffic exhaust and cigarette smoke from pedestrians huddled together at bus stops. Holding her daughter's small, light hand, the removed feeling of watching herself, the suspension between realities begins to dissipate, but the genesis of it—this terror about her father still in her chest—*Be careful not to scare yourself,* David keeps telling her. Still. What should she tell herself? *Look what happened with Fiona! Look what happened when James called!*

"Mommy, shout out the chimes with me!" The cathedral bells of St. John's ring in the distance, and Fiona calls out, "One o'clock! Two o'clock! Three o'clock, Four o'clock! Shout it with me, Mommy!"

Nora wills herself to count, wills herself to stay present. They shout out, "Five o'clock, six o'clock, seven o'clock, eight o'clock!" *This is who I am,* she thinks. *A mother with her daughter, walking to school, singing to the bells. Everything will be all right.*

They arrive at Lowell Elementary School. Red-cheeked children run around the lawn near the entrance, all boots and mittens and hats leaping on crusted piles of dirty snow, making snowballs that fall apart as soon as they throw them. Mothers and fathers, grandparents and neighbors cluster on the sidewalk, keeping an eye on their children and gossiping until the bell rings. As Nora and Fiona get close, heads spin. Stare. A few parents greet Nora awkwardly but turn quickly away. Karen Matthews glares at Nora in such a way that heat slides across Nora's face like another skin, slides down her neck, and pools in the space between her breasts. Matthews is the volunteer coordinator for the school district and knows everything about everyone. Of course she knows about Nora's leave of absence. Even though Bill Guenther didn't press charges and it's been kept out of the paper, Capitol Hill is a tight community. They all know by now.

The bell rings. Phil Johnson walks by her, holding his son's hand. He whispers in her ear, "Guenther's an asshole. Good for you."

"Come say hi to Ms. Monica," Fiona says, tugging on Nora's hand. "You haven't seen her in forever! And also, guess what?"

"What, honey?"

"She's having a baby!"

"She is?" Nora has missed things. She'd stopped walking Fiona to school weeks ago when Paul insisted he wanted the extra time with Fiona, insisted she get more rest.

Once they are in the kindergarten classroom, Fiona runs to hang up her coat and put away her lunch box. A very pregnant Monica in a flowery flannel dress walks over to Nora, takes her hand, and squeezes. "Nora, it's been ages. How *are* you?"

Monica knows. Nora can see it in her eyes.

"I've been better," she says. And for a moment, considers saying more, considers saying, "I'm losing my mind and the world is such a fucked-up place," but Monica is young, and hope and innocence are growing inside her.

Monica lowers her voice, tucks a bunch of her long brown hair behind an ear. "I'm . . . umm . . . sorry about what happened." Her cheeks flush pink, and she nervously runs her hand across her round belly. "That must have been terrible."

Nora nods, turns to watch Fiona, who is carrying a red bucket of chalk over to a small easel in the corner.

"And then that girl—the girl who killed herself? God. Did you know her?"

"Yes," Nora says in a low voice, keeping her eyes focused on her daughter. "A beautiful girl, gone." She turns back to the young woman, looks in her wide, green eyes. "Don't think of these things now, honey," she says. "You're having a baby, a perfect miracle." She reaches out to touch the pregnant belly but quickly stops, her hand hanging there like a frozen bird, but Monica takes her hand then and places it firmly on herself, startling Nora into a panic—she doesn't want to dirty it, the child, she doesn't want to dirty the child, jerks the hand away again and Monica's eyes are hurt and confused, but now Fiona is here, grabbing her other hand, "Mommy, come see the bug house!" and Nora saying to Monica, "Forgive me," and here's the bug house and then the bell and finally she can get out of here, but on the way home the words *"Dad's here"* close in and she has to run, she has to run, she has to run.

The clank and bang of the ferry terminals and the waves slamming against pilings and gulls squawking so tortuously loud she covers her ears and the street's already crowded with tourists, all of them staring at her, pity plastered across their faces, and she runs faster until she sees up ahead the old man who squats near the Starbucks doorway each day, the one with the opaque eyes who strums quiet on his guitar, a bottle of vodka lying at his side like a dazed girlfriend. When Nora is near him, she stops and leans against the brick wall, slides her hands from her ears, and allows the music to absorb her, the mauve notes and delicate arcs and spirals soften and ease her mind, and slowly she becomes more herself. The music hypnotic, carrying her back to her grandfather.

Sundays, her grandfather played his accordion on the sidewalk in front of Paddy Mac's Bar, a hand-rolled smoke dangling from his mouth, the limestone waters of Loch Measca in the background. "La Castagnari," he'd say in an Italian accent to tourists asking about the accordion, and he would show them how with a single button he made one note on the draw and another on the pull. And she would sit on the bench, watching, his hands yellowed and weathered from years of tilling and pulling and coaxing impotent Irish dirt to render, to yield something into his hands. His fingers skittering over buttons, notes flying fast over the loch, the bogs, the way he compressed and expanded the bellows, allowing its breath, its vibrations made sounds inside her body. Sometimes he'd lay the accordion on her lap. His huge hands guiding her small ones through leather straps, pressing her fingers on the buttons. "What do you feel?" he'd ask, and she'd shrug she didn't know. "Do you feel green like tangled ivy or yellow as the hawthorn blossom or black like the raven?" he'd ask and wink at her and make her laugh. And when she'd tell him her color, he'd show her the buttons that created the color, and she'd play feelings she couldn't even imagine.

A teenager yells to the old man, "Rock it, dude!" and startles Nora, but no matter, she is slightly better now. As she walks away, she floats a dollar into the old man's guitar case, and he gives her a wink, and she smiles back. Along the boardwalk a young woman with a diamond in her nose and bleached white hair spiking wildly out of her head sells white freesias and red anemones from a little cart. Nora chooses the red anemones.

"They're beautiful, yes?" the woman says.

"Resurrection," Nora whispers.

"Huh?" the woman says, plucking the flowers from their metal pails with her long fingers, the word LUCK tattooed across her knuckles, silver rings covering half of each finger.

Quietly and slowly, because she still feels disturbed from all the emotions of the morning but is determined to work her way back to normal, Nora tells her the story of Adonis and Aphrodite, how the two young lovers had gone hunting and how a wild boar gored Adonis to death, and Aphrodite sprinkled nectar on his wounds, and crimson anemones sprung up where each drop of his blood had fallen.

The woman wraps the dripping anemones carefully in newspaper and passes them to Nora, her black eyes kind and attentive. "Thank you," she says. "Take care."

But then at home, James pleading on the answering machine, *"Please Nora, just talk to him. Please."* An unexpected deep ache rises within her chest. Perhaps she should talk to him—but her body tightens then. "Jesus," she says aloud. And she goes to lie down, but there, on her pillow, a dusty pink candy heart. KISS ME, it says.

She stares at it. *It's only a sweet gift from Fiona,* her mind tells her. Yet—here is her throat locking up, a punch of danger to her gut. The banging of her heart fills the room. *No, please, not again. Please no.*

Behind her a man says, "Nora?" She turns and looks.

"Daddy!" she jumps up, so happy to see him! He enters the room, smiling, closes the door behind him, walks toward her, smiling, still wearing his work clothes, his brown suit and green tie. *"Happy Valentine's Day, Princess,"* he says. He sits on the bed, takes her hand. *"Daddy! Look at my new red dress! From Ireland! It's my Valentine's dress!"* She twirls around in front of him, and he claps his hands together, smiling. But then, there is something wrong—something is wrong with his smile,
   something is wrong
   with his blue eyes.
   His blue eyes too shiny.
   And his forehead sweaty.
   "Are you sick Daddy?"
   and she loosens his tie,
   the way he's taught her,
   the way she does it each night
   for him when he comes home.
   "No princess."
   He pats the bed, says,

"Sit by me."
She climbs up next to him.
Breathing aftershave and money.
"I have something for you," he says,
and he holds a pink candy heart close to her
face.
Asks her
to read the words.
She looks at him,
unsure
of his eyes,
his voice.
"Say it," he says.
"Kiss me," she says, barely a whisper,
and he leans in and kisses her
softly on the lips.
And he pops the candy in her mouth
his hand on her leg,
stroking.
stroking.
stroking.
"Your Valentine's dress is so pretty," he says.
"A princess in a fairy tale," he says.
When he lifts her on top of him things spin
in her mind, his breathing goes deep, and she
clenches her hands, fingernails digging into her
skin. Everything is wrong.
"Say it again," her daddy whispers,
now moving her
back and forth

back and forth slow
back and forth fast
on his lap
making sounds she doesn't know
and when she doesn't speak,
can't speak
he says,
"Say it, say, 'Kiss me, kiss me,' "
*A*nd she hears Sister Rosa then, hears her say, *"Be brave!"* but she is too frightened to be brave and Sister Rosa says, *"Pray. Pray to St. Margaret."* Her father's hand up her Valentine's dress, burning between her legs and she prays, *St. Margaret, please, please help me, please take me away,* and over his shoulder, her blurred eyes stare at the wallpaper, one white lamb, two orange kittens, three yellow chicks, one white lamb, two orange kittens, three yellow chicks, and she imagines herself into the pictures, one white lamb, two orange kittens, three yellow chicks, one pink girl, but now she is going away, her legs, her arms and hands and fingers, her face, and now there is no color and now there are no sounds and now there is—

—nothing at all.

The phone rings then, startles Nora. It rings and rings, and finally her hands lift the phone, bring it to her ear, and she hears James. James saying things to her out of the answering machine:

"Nora, Dad's in a nursing home. Please Nora, just talk to him." James acting as if everything is fine now, Daddy's fine now, and then on the phone: her father's deep voice—*"Nora? Nora?"* His voice stops her blood. How close he sounds, how familiar, as though he's never been gone, as though nothing has happened.

Her only thought is to run.

She drops the phone and runs down the stairs, runs out the front door, runs down the sidewalk, runs across the bridge. She runs with the intensity of the pursued, through faces and bodies, red lights and sirens. An icy rain pelts down, and within moments, her clothes are soaked through, and her face drips rain. She is drowning, has fallen overboard, swallowed by an omnipotent, lightless sea. Lungs burn, water surges through her, heart closing. She is screaming, "No! No! No!" when the car slams into her. Slams into her body, slams her to the pavement hard.

CHAPTER TWENTY-ONE
THE MORNING OF FEBRUARY 6, 1997

She awakens in a fog and doesn't know where she is. A florescent light flickers above, a slight medicine smell, a TV, a strange room. *A hospital. Oh, God.* A jagged pain rips through her head. Something wrapped tightly around it. She raises her hand to touch it, more pain—an IV stuck in her skin shocks her—*God.* She looks at her body. Sees a pale yellow cotton gown she doesn't recognize.
Shit. What happened?

"Mrs. Brown?"

Nora turns to the voice. A heavyset woman in her late fifties, overpermed hair dyed a fake red, white roots a perfect stripe down the middle. She is wearing a blue uniform and a white plastic name tag that says CAROL. She sits in a chair by her, sets a clipboard down on the nightstand by the bed, and touches Nora's head, takes her blood pressure and pulse, records the information on her clipboard. Shines a light in her eyes with a small flashlight. "I think the morphine must be wearing off darlin'," she says. "We'll give you a bit more in just a little while."

Nora struggles to sit up, pain shooting everywhere. She opens her mouth to speak, but words don't come out. Nothing.

"Now, don't worry about not being able to talk," Carol says, placing ice chips on Nora's lips. "It happens sometimes after a concussion. You'll be fine. Your vitals are good. You have a gash on your head and few bruised ribs, but those will heal up before you know it." She wipes the melted water from Nora's mouth. "Doctor Brinkley will be in to see you later. She's been taking care of you for the last few days, so not to worry. One of Seattle's best."

Nora blinks rapidly. *Last few days?*

"Do you remember anything, darlin'?"

Nora's eyes panicked and watering.

Carol applies another ice chip. "Some guy nearly ran you over."

WHAT?

"Four days ago. Over on Forty-Seventh Street. The jerk didn't even stick around. You were real lucky someone found you and called 911. Though they didn't stick around, either." Carol shakes her head. "Hard to say what's wrong with people these days, they're so afraid and such." She pats Nora's hand. "You could have died if that driver had been going any faster. As it was, he mostly just knocked you off your feet, knocked you out for awhile." She walks to the window and yanks open the curtains. "Good news is you got an east-facing room. Lots of morning light. Did you know that patients stay an average of 3.67 days less in east-facing rooms?" She goes into the bathroom, comes back with a Dixie cup of water. Brings it to Nora's lips.

"Once you can talk again, Doctor Brinkley will ask you all kinds of things—see what you remember and what you don't. You know, like, are you married, do you have kids, who's the president, that kind of thing."

Fuckfuckfuck.

"Of course, I know you have a husband. And a daughter—Fiona is it? They've come in every day, and your brother, James, too, but we can't let them in until you're cleared by Dr. Brinkley."

James? James was here? And then she remembers—her father—her father's voice on the phone. Her body goes immediately stiff. *Oh, God, please don't let my father be here. No, no, no, please no.* And adrenaline shoots and her heart races then and her throat tightens. She can't breathe and she twists and jerks and now the car slams into her, cracking her open, and the needle rips out, kiss me, kiss me my princess, and she shrieks but there are no sounds, and Carol murmuring and now the needle in her arm and again swimming, swimming, swimming in the cold and she can't keep her head above water.

CHAPTER TWENTY-TWO
THE AFTERNOON OF FEBRUARY 6, 1997

Nora lies staring at the drip, drip, drip of the IV: the clear liquid trickles down the tube into the needle; the needle pierces the vein. *Don't think about him. Don't think about him. Don't think about him.* She tries not to think about him, but she can't stop thinking about him.

And now Carol brings her breakfast, encourages her to sit by the window, puts the plastic tray on her lap, says this is such a nice room for morning coffee because of the early sunlight, reminds her with a wink about the luck of an east-facing room, and leaves her, says she'll be back soon. Nora holds onto the tray. Out the window a girl catches snowflakes on her tongue, but now the girl's tongue becomes her own tongue on the skin of her father, and now the wheezing of a bus becomes the wheezing of his body on her body and she braces herself for impact and the tray crashes to the floor and she doesn't know what is true and what is not, and now Carol is here stroking her hair saying everything will be all right, holding out a pink pill saying, "Here, darlin', take this." And Nora is tired of horror flicks in her mind, tired of the smells and sounds of him and opens her mouth and Carol says,

"Okay, yes, darlin'," and folds the pink pill into Nora's hand and offers a tiny paper cup of water with her other hand, and Nora places the pill into her mouth and swallows the water but the pill is too large and suddenly she is trying to swallow him and she gags and chokes and Carol has to thump her hard on the back until the pill shoots like a bullet from her mouth. And Carol holds her tightly, coos to her, inches her back to bed and covers her up, tells her *these things happen, flashbacks happen, darlin', and oh, you wouldn't believe the flashbacks her son Daniel had the first year he returned from Iraq.* "You wouldn't believe it," Carol says over and over again until it is a song in Nora's head, a lullaby soothing her breath back to normal.

There is a tapping at the door then, and a tall, fit-looking woman wearing a white uniform walks into the room. Black hair pulled back into a high ponytail, tiny pearls in her ears. She strides over to Nora and thrusts out her hand, the nails unpolished yet perfectly manicured; no-nonsense nails: "Dr. Jean Brinkley."

Nora can only stare back, numb, raises her hand slightly in slow motion. Dr. Brinkley shakes her hand and sets it down gently, studying Nora's face the whole time. She pulls up a chair and starts right in. Carol tiptoes past her, whispers something, and disappears out the door.

"Mrs. Brown, I'm the psychiatrist here at

187

Seattle General. I'll be part of the team working with you and Dr. Forrester for as long as you are with us."

Team? I need a team?

"We don't have any reason to believe you have internal bleeding, so there's no need for a CT or MRI at this point. However, we'd like to keep you for another few days just to be sure—and, well, regarding your inability to talk, we thought we'd wait and see what your therapist recommends.

"Your husband suggested, Mrs. Brown . . . he seems to think, well, he seems to think you may have stepped out in front of the car on purpose. And then, with your reaction last night—until we know more, we've placed you on a seventy-two hour watch. We'll check in on you every ten to fifteen minutes, and with the exception of your therapist and the psychiatric team, no one else will be allowed to visit—for now." As if she sees the confusion in Nora's eyes, she says, "It's the best thing, Mrs. Brown. Please. Trust us."

Nora opens her mouth. Forms a *"No"* with her lips. Breathes hard into the *"No."* She hears the air moving, feel her lungs push it out, but something shoves back into her throat, and there are no words, no words, no words, no words.

"Now," says Dr. Brinkley, touching Nora gently on her arm. "I'd like to ask you a few questions about problems or difficulties you are having.

You may refuse to answer any question or end the interview at any time. The information you give me will be kept confidential. I'll be making notes as we go along." She pauses. Studies Nora. "Do you feel up to that?"

Nora nods.

"I realize you aren't able to speak, but perhaps you can write your answers?" She hands Nora a small pad of paper and a pen. "Shall we begin?"

Nora nods again.

"What's your date of birth?"

Nora writes. Her fingers thick as bricks because of the pink pill. She finally holds the notebook up for Dr. Brinkley to see: **March 4, 1958**.

"Where do you live?"

234 Pike Street.

"Who is the president?"

Clinton.

"Name three rivers."

Mississippi, Columbia, Elwha.

"What does 'bull in a china shop' mean?"

Acting clumsy.

"Do you have any children? If so, how many, and what are their names?"

Oh, God, Fiona. What does she know? She must be so frightened. It's hard to make the pen move. She aches for Fiona.

"Mrs. Brown? Do you have any children?"

She writes, her hand advancing in slow motion.

One, Fiona, age 6.

"What kind of work do you do?"

High school English teacher.

"Why are you here?"

Her gut tightens. Her bruised ribs ache, and the ache moves into her hand. She will write anyway. She needs to get the hell out of here.

Hit by a car.

"Why were you in the middle of the street in the dark?"

Upset. Running.

She feels sick. The questions are oppressive—she considers writing "because I'm insane"; "because my husband's having an affair"; "because my father whom I haven't seen in twenty-seven years is back"; "because I remember what happened when I wore the Valentine's dress." But she can't. She feels like she might begin stabbing Dr. Brinkley with the pen.

"Mrs. Brown—can you tell me why you were upset?"

This is all too complicated and dangerous. She writes: **Can't you just look in David's reports?**

She throws the pen and paper on the bedside table. Closes her eyes. Takes deep breaths.

"Okay. Okay. Just rest now. But I'm going to tell you something. And I'm telling you to help you. Okay?"

Nora stays still.

"There are people who would rather be here, you know, in a hospital, than admit something traumatic happened to them. I know that sounds harsh, but it's true. We can help you, and if you let us help, you could walk right out of here."

When Nora says nothing, doesn't open her eyes, Dr. Brinkley says, "So, okay. Your doctor is expected shortly. Would you like me to call Carol, have her sit with you until he arrives?"

Nora shakes her head. She feels suddenly ashamed.

"There's a struggle going on inside you," David says quietly. "A struggle between you and that little girl." David sits in the chair by her bed. She is propped up against pillows, eyes closed. Listening to him.

He is talking kindly, sympathetically, wants to know what happened, saying she'll talk again, this must be so hard, what a relief talking can be—the way it puts distance between you and the pain, that she'll talk when she's ready. She opens her eyes and looks fixedly at him. She wants to tell him why she ran, why this isn't right, that she needs to go home, that she doesn't know if she was trying to kill herself. She doesn't know. She tries again to speak. Silence.

"There's nothing to be ashamed of," he is saying. "Could we discuss last night?"

She nods.

"Did you think about something in particular, or did a thought come to you when you didn't expect it?" He hands her the notebook and pen.

She stares and stares at the blank page. Brain cells frozen, then frenetic. Her hand lifts the pen as if it will write something but then drops shakily to her side.

"It's safe here," David says. "You're safe. Say what you want to say. You are no longer under his roof."

She can't.

"You've been guarding this secret for a lifetime, Nora," he says gently. "You don't have to anymore. You don't need to. It's the secrets that make us sick; it's the telling that heals."

The repercussions. The shame of everyone knowing the truth of her. And what will happen to her father? How can she do this to him? But now, here is the hand, fierce and steady, stabbing, stabbing, stabbing words into the notebook right before her eyes.

I remember the Valentine's dress. Margaret is telling the truth.

And now, it is all too much. This telling. This remembering. She closes her eyes and curls her body tight and braces herself for the objects and words that fly hard into walls, against her face, curling tighter and tighter until she disappears.

CHAPTER TWENTY-THREE
FEBRUARY 7, 1997

By the time David arrives the next day, Nora's emotions have fallen off the edge. She writes a note in panic, rips it out, and gives it to him with a trembling hand.

I need to get out of here. Please. I want to go home.

He exhales sympathetically. "I know you've remembered something horrific." He touches her arm gently. "We need to work through this. In a safe place. I think you should stay, at least until you can assure yourself—and me—that you can keep yourself safe."

She grounds herself in his eyes. *Am I a danger to others? And why the hell isn't my voice coming back?*

"Your brother was here earlier. He doesn't want you to worry about your father. He wants to see you. He said your father didn't come with him—he stayed in Rochester. He wants you to know your father is not physically capable of travel, nor, he said, emotionally able. 'Weak and ineffectual, as always,' he said."

She should feel relieved, but she isn't—she feels a surge of nausea, anxiety swelling, heads of penises edging their way in—she

193

fights to follow her breath, to stay present.

"You wrote that you remembered the Valentine's dress, that Margaret is telling the truth," David says. He's decided on a new direction. And then ever so carefully, he says, "Nora, did your father hurt you?"

Her eyes well. Her father. Her daddy. She'd loved him. She'd hated him. She'd loved him more than anyone. She'd loved him more than anything.

"Your father?" he asks.

She nods. Tears come then.

He sits there with her, silently, for a long time. As Dr. Brinkley and Carol come and go with their stethoscopes and pills and worried faces, he stays. He stays and wipes her tears and sits by her in silence until she stops crying.

He takes her hand. "Nora, when your father abused you, you were a child. You couldn't make sense of what was happening to you. Let me tell you something. When I was a child, I lived in San Francisco. One day there was a tremendous earthquake. The first earthquake I'd ever experienced—a 7.0. I was terrified. I was home alone with my father, and I thought we would die. Everything shook and crashed. An entire wall of our house crumbled in front of our eyes. I sat bundled into my father, the two of us curled up in the bathtub. I couldn't stop shaking. I felt him shaking. When things finally quieted, we sat for awhile, not moving. Not talking. And then he turned me so he could look me in the eyes and said, 'That was an earthquake. We're okay,' and then we talked about it until I stopped shaking."

She gazes vacantly out the window. Searches for the silver of Puget Sound between sky-scrapers. There it is. The mountains a snowy wall in the distance. She presses her face to the glass; the wire mesh behind it makes her feel like she's in a confessional.

"Nora," David says, even more softly, "a child who is sexually abused doesn't have someone nearby naming what happened, saying *that was sexual abuse and that's a crime.* Your father did a horrible thing to you and is very, very sick. He had no right to do such a thing. Do you hear what I'm saying? When you can't name a trauma, or speak about it—"

Is there a name for what my father did?

"Love," her father had said. "This is love."

CHAPTER TWENTY-FOUR
FEBRUARY 8, 1997

Nora wakes up in a different room. She's still in the hospital—with its scoured air and slack light, but this room has an eerie, lonely feeling about it, and a ripple of panic sweeps through her. The IV is gone, but where her hand rests, a white cotton strap—a restraint—hangs from the metal railing of the bed. She reaches up and finds the gauze has been removed from her head.

"They've moved you, Nora." It is David. He sits in the deep windowsill, a white blizzard outside behind him. With his white hair and white beard, everything white, she thinks wildly that maybe she'd been in a goddamned nightmare, and now the white will swallow up the darkness and she'll wake up with the horrible ordeal behind her.

"You woke up last night, hysterical, and when they couldn't calm you, they medicated you and moved you here—it's a quieter room."

Down the hall a woman screams. A murmuring of voices rush by. She's not going to be rescued by the white. She's in the One Flew over the Cuckoo's Nest ward.

David pulls up a chair next to her. "You are in the psychiatric unit of the hospital. Dr. Brinkley, Paul, and I thought—"

But her actions stop his words as she struggles to sit up, her ribs still aching. She grabs a notebook from the bedside table and writes angrily.

Paul?

"Nora, when the hospital told him they couldn't hold you any longer in the emergency unit, he called me, and well—after last night's trauma, we spoke on the phone and decided this would be best."

The sting of Paul making this decision fuels her temper. Her face burning, she writes with trembling fingers: **I do NOT need to be here. I want to go home.**

She aches for her daughter, wants to wrap her arms around her, even hear her giggle about the upcoming Valentine's Day party. Erase old memories. Make new ones.

"I know this is hard," David says, "but it's really important you rest—that nothing, no one, triggers another crisis—that you get your voice back."

Will I ever get better?

"Listen," he says, leaning in, his brown eyes warm and clear. "The fact that you remembered the Valentine's dress while you were awake is huge. The splitting of your mind was, and is, a brilliant coping mechanism. Your brain's entire physiology changed so you could endure what happened and go on living your life. As a child you had no control over your body. And ever since that time, you *have* been in control. You've had control over emotions that may have overwhelmed you, overwhelmed anyone, saved your life. And now, you've remembered something—something that could mean your brain is attempting to integrate—heal the splitting. That's huge. Remember when we talked about looking for patterns and images that could give us clues to your past? Those images are linking. It's like finding the missing beads for your rosary. It means—" he hesitates.

She mouths, "What?"

"Some incest victims survive by ignoring what the perpetrator did—by refusing to believe it. They come to me again and again telling me they are crazy—and believing it—coming to me with addiction issues, relationship issues, week after week, until finally, some of them admit to the truth of their past. Margaret is your truth. Which is why it's possible," he says, "that the integration will include Margaret."

You mean she might go away?

"Yes, potentially."

But he has barely uttered the word when the thinning door in her mind begins to slide, slide, slide shut and she drops the notebook and the silence spreads and she is gone.

"Nora wants me to go away?" says a small, tearful voice.

"Margaret? Margaret, is that you?"

She tries to pull the blanket over her head, but Nora's bruised ribs are hurting her, and it's hard, but she gets it over herself. Once she's all the way covered, she listens for where he is.

"Margaret?"

He sounds too close. "Could you please move away from me?" she says, her voice barely a whisper.

He screeches his chair back.

"How's this?"

She peeks out of the blanket. "A little more."

He backs up another few feet. After a minute he says, "Margaret, thank you for coming," and then, gently, "Is there something you want to tell me?"

"Please," she says, "could you please lock the door?"

"We can't lock the door, but everyone has promised to stay outside unless I call them in. You are very safe here."

She will keep being brave. She will talk to him.

"Margaret, did you come to help Nora?"

"I hate Nora. I hate her," she says louder than is safe and she forgets to keep the blanket over her head and she sees him see her.

"No one will hurt you, Margaret. No one."

She wiggles back under the blanket now. She will stay hiding.

"Margaret, why do you hate Nora?"

She shouts in a tremulous voice from under the covers. "You know why! Nora broke us! She ran us in front of a car and the car slammed us and broke our chest and banged our head and we had a mean needle in our hand and she's not speaking and now . . ."

"And now?"

"And now we can't help Fiona!"

"Fiona? Why does Fiona need help?"

"Oh, this is bad!" she says beginning to rock, the blankets quivering. "So bad. It's almost Valentine's Day, oh no, oh no, this is so bad, sobadsobadsobad."

"Margaret, what is so bad? Please, please tell me."

"Paul was telling Fiona the princess words," she whispers. Her heart is going very fast now. "He keeps saying, 'My little princess, my little princess,' and it's almost Valentine's Day and we have to help Fiona!"

"Margaret. It will be okay. I will help Fiona, okay? I promise, but you have to help me."

"How?"

"Can you tell me if Fiona's daddy has hurt her before?"

She will try very hard now. She brings her head above the covers, nervously glances at the door, and then looks right at him, blinking rapidly.

"I don't know, but he says the princess words and she has tummy aches and when daddies say the princess words, next come the candy hearts that say *'Kiss me'* and the big hand and 'kiss me, kiss me' and the hurting and 'You are my princess' and then a new pink bike with rainbow streamers and a Barbie and a doll house and more *'kiss me, kiss me'* and Nora isn't there to watch out and oh no, oh no, oh no . . .'"

Margaret's insides are fluttering, and there is a glump, glump, glumping in her ears. David is *not* acting like this is an emergency. She needs to get to Fiona. Even though Nora has teached and teached Fiona to say "NO!" to bad touching, daddies can be very, very tricky and bad. She tries to throw the blankets off her body, but the ribs hurt her too hard—

"Margaret!"

She stops frozen because David is standing up and moving to her—*Oh, no. Oh, no. I am a stupid, stupid girl.* She makes herself very small and very still, very still, very still. *Please don't hurt me, please don't hurt me.*

He stops moving. "Margaret. Please. You are safe. But if you try to get out of that bed again, you will hurt yourself more, and it will take longer to see Fiona."

She looks at him. He has stopped. He is not going to hurt her. She will listen. Even if he is tricking her, he is right. She will be quiet with her body. She will use only her mouth. "You need to help Fiona right now!"

"Okay, Margaret. I will. He walks to the coat rack and plucks his raincoat from the hook. "I would like to say goodbye to Nora first. Will you help me with that?"

Margaret is sitting straight up now, eyes wide. "Yes, but the biggest thing is to remind Fiona of how to dial the 911 and to bring the phone close to her and there is one on the dresser and it has a long cord you can stretch and stretch all the way to her bed. Nora showed her how to use it. And . . . and . . . tell her for sure to call it when she's scared and tell her about all the bad touching things again." She begins rocking, rocking, saying, "You will do that right?"

"Yes. I will absolutely do that. I will go as soon as I talk to Nora. And Margaret?"

"What?"

"You are so very brave and I am really sorry your daddy hurt you. What he did was horribly wrong. He had no right to do that to you. He was very sick."

She doesn't stop rocking, whispers, "Will you please go now to check on Fiona?"

"I will call Nora's doctor and leave a note for you as soon as I know about Fiona, okay?"

"Okay," and she closes her eyes so he will leave faster.

Nora is pulled from the deep gray silence and opens her eyes and struggles to know where she is and if she's in a dream or not. She sees David and smells the room and remembers. Worry slides across his face, and her stomach tightens with what he might say.

He tells her Margaret spoke to him, "Which means," he says, carefully, "that your not being able to speak *is* psychological."

But all she wants to know is: **What did she say?**

He stares at the note for a few moments and says slowly, "She thinks . . . she thinks Paul may be abusing Fiona."

Her eyes shout "What!" His words turning the room red. She needs to get out of this damn bed and go home. She struggles with the covers, her movements still limited because of the bruised ribs, and realizes suddenly she is wearing only a hospital gown. Her arms cross over her chest.

Without hesitating, David goes to the closet and comes back with her robe. "Paul brought it yesterday," he says. "Your brother was with him; Fiona was in school. They brought a whole suitcase of clothes for you."

Paul and James were here? She wraps the white robe around her tightly, reaches for the belt, but it's not there.

"Belts aren't allowed, Nora. Sorry."

Out the window, feathery snowflakes fall so thick and heavy, all she can see is white. Fiona's words burst into her mind: "The angels are sifting

203

flour from heaven! It's like we're in a snow globe, Mommy!"

If the window weren't locked, if it didn't have this wire mesh, she might jump. She might. She could jump into the thick, slow silence and kill her body, kill her madness.

She begins shaking her head, no, no, no, slowly at first, then faster and faster until David is there, hands on her shoulders, shuffling her toward a chair, asking her to please sit down, please breathe in, breathe out.

She tries to speak, but there is only a small frightening sound, her mouth stiff and useless. She shakes her head again, no, no, no. Paul would *never* hurt his daughter. Never. His life, fast and aggressive to her, every moment an opportunity to make money, climb a ladder, strike a deal over cognac. He's been hungrier for power, more ravenous for status than she'd expected. And she's turned her back on his world, made him angry. But NO, he would never hurt Fiona.

"Nora, there really is nothing you've told me to suggest Paul would hurt Fiona in this way. Have you ever seen him display affection that is inappropriate?"

She shakes her head no.

But she thinks now about how insistent she'd been with Paul, that it was her, not him, who would give Fiona baths. Paul had thought this unreasonable, but as with most of their parenting decisions, had shrugged it off as her decision. She'd not understood her own insistence or the vague anxiety that wound around it. Had she sensed something unconsciously?

"And there are signs, you know?" he says. "Like sexual preoccupation in her play or language or drawings, inserting toys into—"

She holds up a hand to stop him from going on. *I know the signs! Have you forgotten I'm a teacher?* Nora's eyes welling. Her head shaking an emphatic "No!" but her mind panicking. God, had she been paying enough attention?

"So let's just stay calm about this," David says. "I'll meet with Paul and Fiona, make sure she's safe."

Yes, she nods, taking deep breaths to slow the fast blinking of her eyes.

"I want to honor Margaret's fears, but I also know—Nora, are you with me?"

She nods.

"Children and adults who have been sexually abused trust very few people, and it takes a long time for them to regain trust—so let's take this a step at a time, okay?"

Her mind is a blur. She needs to get to Fiona. She paces, frantic short breaths jarring the quiet room, playing and replaying conversations with Fiona: good touching, bad touching, good secrets, and bad secrets. Was it enough? Is that why Paul asked for more time alone with Fiona, took so long to tuck her in at night, was he really only reading her stories? Her ribs stabbing now. Oh, God, it hurts, it hurts, it hurts, now arms around her, it is David, laying her down on the bed.

He touches her arm. "I'll check on her," he says. "Right now. Do you hear me?"

Yes, yes, she nods, takes a deep breath, and closes her eyes.

"Nora, I need to tell Paul what's going on. I'll need to tell him about Margaret—probably best to tell James, too. Are you alright with that?"

He studies her face with unwavering eyes. She returns his look, unblinking, and at last she nods yes.

CHAPTER TWENTY-FIVE
FEBRUARY 11, 1997

"Someone sent flowers," Carol says, handing Nora a bouquet of yellow sweetheart roses.

Nora takes the flowers and breathes in the delicate smell. Once Carol leaves, she pulls out the tiny white card stuck between the stems and lays the flowers on her chest. They're from John.

I know you're not seeing visitors yet, but I wanted you to know I'm thinking of you. The kids miss you. I miss you. Be well soon. Call me if you want.

She misses John. He is the only one she can talk to with complete freedom. He listens without trying to correct or fix. She can say anything she wants, and it's all right.

"I believe Fiona is safe," David says, entering the hospital room then, breaking her reverie. He takes his coat off and hangs it on the metal rack by the door. She reaches over and places the flowers in her water glass.

"Nora," he says, genuine concern in his voice, "I really think she's safe."

Anxiety and relief distort her breath. She reaches for her notebook and pen, but before she can write anything, he says, "I'm going to keep meeting with her, for at least a couple of weeks and longer if necessary, but honestly, I think she's okay. We talked and played for over an hour and she was quite animated—I didn't see or hear anything to suggest she's troubled about something. She's worried about you, of course."

Her eyes close. She can see Fiona sitting cross-legged on the couch in David's office answering questions, biting her lip at first, her face scrunched with the effort to help.

"With each question I asked," he says, "she relaxed more, and after awhile, it seemed she'd forgotten why she was there at all. She described all the fun she has with her daddy: riding the trolley to the aquarium and the library, listening to ball games on the radio, making pancakes in animal and heart shapes on Saturday mornings, and she didn't talk in a way that suggested she was protecting him—I know that voice, Nora. She was very open—very unlike a child who is keeping a terrible secret. In fact, she told me all about the Valentine's party coming up at school, and how excited she was to have James staying with them. This is all a good sign. If she'd been hurt, especially in the last few days, she would have been withdrawn or anxious, and frankly, I really doubt she'd have agreed to being left alone with me at all. Most abusers create an enmeshment where the child has no real sense of self—quite the opposite of Fiona. She seems very clear about her feelings and opinions—Nora, are you listening?"

She opens her eyes and turns to him. Caught somewhere between past and present.

"Nora, I was saying Fiona seems to have an incredibly strong separate self."

An incredibly strong separate self. Nora thinks of a time not too long ago when she and Fiona had been shopping at Macy's. Fiona had stopped in front of a full-length mirror, flexed her muscles like she'd often seen Paul do, and said, "I'm really strong, aren't I, Mommy?" and Nora had smiled and said, "No question about that, darling! You're a warrior goddess!" Fiona had walked a little closer to the mirror, brushed her wispy blonde bangs to the side, and said in a surprised voice, "And my eyes are so pretty," her breath leaving a tiny blur of steam on the mirror. Nora had stood behind Fiona then, wrapped her arms around her. Her daughter so confident, so different than Nora had been as a child.

"You are the most beautiful little girl in the world, baby."

"Mommy!" Fiona said, "I am *not* a baby!" And Nora had been startled, filled with sadness, realizing that indeed, Fiona was no longer a baby, that someday she would lose her.

David waits for a response, but when there is none, he says, "And the fact Paul had no qualms about me interviewing Fiona without him in the room is also a positive sign. He was really hurt by the accusation, that was clear, but I have to tell you, most of the abusive parents I've had contact with rarely allow an interview without protest or court order. Most will do anything to keep their inner circle private, protected."

Even though she hadn't believed Paul would ever hurt Fiona, right now in this moment, she trusts David's perceptions more than her own. And James is with Fiona now too—he will know if something is wrong, he will watch out for her. She turns to look out the window, blinking away tears of frustration and confusion. The city lost in the blizzard—she can barely see two inches in front of her. *Most will do anything to keep their inner world private. Protected.*

And then, suddenly, her father, in her mind. How he didn't believe in play dates; birthday parties; slumber parties; Halloween, with its masks and trickery; friends coming over. Not that she had any. Not that anyone in their family had any. Definitely no one had a "sense of a separate self." She remembers too, how, except for the hours he worked and she attended school, she only wanted to be with him. A collage of images then: her in pajamas, sitting on the green porcelain bathtub watching him shave, so handsome in the mirror, the familiar smell of him; her organizing his tools in the basement while he built things—him lifting her up on the workbench to hang his wrenches, screwdrivers, and hammers on the pegboard; dancing after dinner in the living room to Patsy Cline while her mother washed dishes; him singing "Tennessee Waltz" to her while she played in the bathtub— her father's voice singing, *"I was waltzing with my darling,"* as he dried her with a big white towel, him kneeling, then humming, humming into her ear, drying her back, her tummy, then breathing, breathing, loud breathing, the towel between her legs, then no towel only hands, his hands touching her. Her hands stiff at her sides. She is him. Her eyes closing. Private. Protected.

From far away, David's voice, "You are safe. I am here. Let the images come, let them come."

Her father's voice whispering, "Our secret, our secret, our secret," the hands rubbing between her legs, hard and fast.

CHAPTER TWENTY-SIX
FEBRUARY 12, 1997

The snow has finally stopped, and the city lays silent and vulnerable, covered thickly in white. An occasional car or person negotiates the steep, frozen hill. Skyscrapers, like icicles, vanish into cumulus clouds. An Ivar's billboard on top of the Nordstrom building reads CLAM CHOWDER WORTH SURFACING FOR! Slices of Puget Sound glimmer between the buildings. Someone is crying down the hall. Someone is always crying down the hall. If the windows weren't nailed shut, she could smell the ocean salt in the air. It is dusk of her tenth day in the psychiatric ward.

"Kind of a pretty picture," David says, as he reaches down to pick up his thermos. He loosens the top and trickles coffee into his cup. He wears what he always wears, jeans and a black T-shirt, except today he also wears a black cardigan. She has on jeans, a slate-gray sweater, and her gray wool slippers—items Paul dropped off the first day she'd arrived. Six days ago, and he hasn't come back since. Perhaps the doctor or David discouraged him, told him she needed to rest. Perhaps he's furious about the accusations. Still, it seems a husband would insist, find a way to see his wife.

She sits there, in the space between sentences, trying to stop thinking about what she knows, but she can't stop thinking about any of it. She's had a nightmarish sleep, images of long fingers, purplish and hard, filling up spaces, making it hard to breathe, waking her in a sweat, the cries and screams of other patients in the background, and she hadn't known then what was real or what was imagined or if someone was dying or not.

He leans forward and looks at her for a moment. "You must be exhausted. This is hard. Really hard." He pauses, says, "And, you released a lot. But give it time, okay? This isn't a process you can rush." He takes his glasses off and cleans them on his shirt hem, puts them on again. "That you even faced the memories indicates a tremendous step forward."

The flashbacks yesterday had terrified her, felt more painful than she thought she could handle, more than she could contain. And yet, she'd survived. Weary and exhausted and strangely lighter. A young woman carrying two grocery bags tramps up the hill. Nora wishes she were the one carrying groceries home, making dinner, Fiona at her side. *Can I go home now? Can I trust myself not to run blindly into the street again?*

"Do you want to talk about yesterday, or would you rather just rest? We don't have to talk about anything today." His voice is cautious.

She looks at him, her hands folded in her lap

on top of the little yellow notebook, the pen stuck into the spiral. She plucks it out, opens the notebook, and writes: **I would like to be alone today. I'd like to look out this window. I'd like to sleep.**

"Okay," David says and stands up to leave.

But then she remembers and has to know, scribbles fast: **Did you tell Paul about Margaret?**

David reads her note, runs a hand through his thick white hair, and looks at her. Sits back down. Finally he says, "He didn't take it well." The lines around his mouth and across his forehead are deeper than she remembers.

After a moment, she writes: **He thinks I'm crazy—like Sybil. It's true, admit it.**

She knows by David's expression she's right, even though he says, "Paul just needs time. This on top of the accusation, I don't know. It's a lot to deal with. And it's not unusual for a spouse to shut down or find fault with the person in crisis. Your pain may have brought up some pain of his he doesn't want to deal with, or he might be someone who's ashamed of having an imperfect life, I have no idea. He didn't want to talk about it."

Down the hall someone plays the radio, a country and western channel. She turns her face to the window. Outside, a man in a red stocking cap and long wool coat stands in the snow and plays a guitar with fingerless gloves. Next to him sits a ruffled Irish wolfhound. The wolfhound faces the musician, its head held high. A small crowd has gathered, and the wolfhound's eyes never leave the musician. Nora wonders if they are listening to the music or just interested in the massive size of the wolfhound or its attentiveness to the musician or all three things.

"Do not for a minute doubt yourself. You're a hero," David says. "You're walking right into the flames to save a self. *Your* self. Do not doubt that for a minute.

"James listened carefully," David says. "But he didn't want to talk about it. He wants to talk to you."

She can see James listening to David, his arms folded across his chest, his face concentrated, trying to understand, trying not to judge, the way he looks at art and things in life he doesn't understand.

She writes: **I need to see all of them. Paul. James. Fiona too. I can't be away from her any longer.**

"Oh, Nora. Jeez. You're taking on a lot. You don't want to wait until your voice comes back?"

I need to see all of them. I want to see Paul first, though—alone. Please. Can you arrange this for me?

"I have to tell you—this may be very difficult. Because Paul isn't in a great place he may lash

215

out, he might trigger something in Margaret. And James—if you decide to talk to James about this, it may be—well, he may not believe you. It was hard to read his face. And sometimes when siblings . . ." he hesitates. "More often than not, siblings turn against the one who breaks the secret—make her feel guilty, crazy, call her a liar. They need to get rid of the ugliness . . . and you're the one who brought it. You're the messenger of a dirtied legacy—"

James wouldn't do that.

"I'm just saying he might feel he has to protect himself. Just be prepared."

Protect himself from what?

"From the fact that his father was a child molester."

I want to see him. I don't want to talk about anything with him right now. I just want to see him.

"Okay, okay. I'll arrange for a visit. And Paul?"

She is silent for a few moments, then writes: **I want to see him.**

"Nora, you're in charge here. If you really want to see him, that's okay. I'll talk to him."

She mouths, "Thank you."

David gets up to leave but remembers something. He pulls a photograph from a file in his backpack, hands it to her. "James asked me to give this to you."

She holds the photo with both hands. A little

girl with blue eyes looks out at her. The girl wearing the Valentine's dress. Nora gasps as if she's just had the wind knocked out of her. She has never seen this picture before.

"She was born with a sacred sense of trust," David says.

Nora stares at the girl for a long time. The blue eyes of her. The truth of her.

"Nora, you did *nothing* to cause his horrific behavior. You could have danced around naked in front of him, and he shouldn't have touched you. He abused you because of the way *he* was, not because of you or your behavior. This isn't about sex. It's about power. It's about control. *His* lack of power. *His* need to control. He derived power from taking what he wanted. He needed that power. And you were an easy target. He didn't just cross boundaries. He obliterated them."

She sets the picture on the windowsill. Picks up her notebook and writes: **She could have run away. She was smart. Why didn't she just run away?**

"Why do you think you didn't?"

I don't know. I was terrified. Where would I go?

She realizes she'd written *I* instead of *she*.

"Nora, I'm going to ask you something. You don't have to answer it if you're not ready."

She fixes her eyes on him.

217

"Do you remember how your father's eyes looked—when he hurt you?"

His eyes. His blue eyes.

It was as if he didn't see me. As if I wasn't there.

David takes the note and reads it. "You weren't," he says. "In short, you didn't exist while he hurt you. As profoundly sad as it is, you were invisible to him."

Invisible. To the man most important to her. Her father.

"He was in his own self-absorbed world. You were—and I know this is hard to hear—"

Nora nods for him to continue, nervous she'll split into Margaret. She wants to hear this for herself.

"You were an object. A way for him to satisfy his need for control, a way to dominate. Even if you had cried out, told him to stop, he probably wouldn't have heard you. He didn't see you. He had no awareness of your pain."

Sweat under her arms, her breasts. Loss kicking her hard in the stomach.

"He broke into your body and stole your sense of self. You knew something was wrong, you knew it felt horrible, but you also knew your father wouldn't do anything horrible to you, so the obvious thing was to blame yourself. To think something was wrong with you and to doubt yourself. He took away your power to trust your own assessment, your own judgment."

218

He broke into your body and stole your sense of self.

Large, cold hand curling tight around the skin of her throat. Heart beating as if she's running hard. Now David's voice calling her name and Carol's voice saying, "Mrs. Brown, Mrs. Brown," and she opens her eyes to see both of them standing above her stricken.

David putting his hand lightly on her upper arm. "It's all right," he says.

Carol smooths her bangs, holds a paper cup of water to her lips.

Nora sips the water. Something on Carol's belt buzzes.

"You okay now, Mrs. Brown?"

Yes, Nora nods, and Carol leaves them there.

David strokes the back of her hand a bit longer and sits back down on his chair. For several moments, they sit quietly. "And yet," he says as if nothing had just happened, as if he was going to say this no matter what, "and yet, you created Margaret. With your last little bit of power, you created her. You created her to feel in control—to feel safe. You did that. Even as a child, you found a way to keep yourself safe."

She looks at the picture again. She had only gone where no one would find her.

"You are the child trying to heal right now— the child who is waiting for you," he says, his voice fading then, sounding farther and farther away until she can hardly hear him at all, until she must close her eyes, until she is gone.

Margaret brings her hands up to her face, covers it. "Fiona's safe?" she asks in an anxious whisper.

"Margaret?"

"Yes."

He slides his chair away from her, which is very nice of him, but she will keep her hands over her face just in case.

"Yes," he says. "I believe she is, but we will keep a close eye on her, and keep talking to her."

"But what about the princess words Paul said?"

"Margaret, I'm sorry, but I can't hear you. Do you think you could move your hands away from your face? I promise I will not move at all."

"Promise—not even a bit?"

"I promise."

She opens her hands slightly and makes just enough space for her words to get out. She will pretend to be brave. "But what about the princess words Paul said to Fiona?"

"Margaret, lots of daddies call their little girls princesses, but they don't hurt them. It's okay to say those words, it really is."

She doesn't know if this is true, but she will believe him because he has believed her.

"Margaret, do you know why Nora isn't talking?"

"It's not her job to tell the bad things." Margaret

closes her eyes and pushes away the scary feelings. "It's my job. I did the bad things. She is the good one, and I'm the bad one." She wipes her eyes. Begins to rock.

"Margaret. Listen. I'm going to keep telling you this until you believe me. You are *not* the bad one. Nora is *not* the bad one. Your father did the bad things. Very, very bad things. You and Nora are the good ones."

Now she is rocking hard and crying hard and tears run down her arms into the sleeves of Nora's sweater.

"May I give you a Kleenex?"

She nods her head, and through her talking space she hears him walk to the sink and pull a tissue from the box. She stops rocking and listens as he walks toward her, her heart beating hard in her ears. He stands right next to her. *He will not hurt me.* She watches as a tissue floats onto her lap. She waits until David is back in his chair. She grabs the Kleenex and presses it to her tears, trying to dry them without him seeing her face.

"I'm scared. I'm really, really scared."

"What's scaring you?"

"Valentine's Day is in two days, and something really bad is going to happen. I know it. I just know it."

"Margaret, you are safe. I promise nothing bad will happen. I would never let anyone hurt you or Nora."

They are silent for a moment, Margaret shivering.

"Margaret, do you think you could help Nora to speak?

"H-h-how?"

"You've done so much work. You've helped so much, and you've been so brave. I wonder if you could let Nora be in charge for awhile—just rest a bit and let her take care of you? If you could trust her."

Margaret is quiet. She tugs at her bangs with both hands. "Yes," she says through her fingers. "I will trust Nora." And then, slowly, Margaret opens her hands all the way and brings them to her lap. Folds them. Looks straight into David's eyes.

"Hi," he says.

"Hi," she says. He will not hurt her. She will not be scared.

"Margaret," he says, his voice catching. "I am proud of you."

"Oh."

"You have opened a door to where the secret was kept for a long time. You have let in the light. And I know at the deepest place in my heart, Nora will take good care of you and Fiona. You will never ever again have to do anything that hurts you. Ever. We will all keep you safe. I promise."

She whispers, "You will call for me if you need me, right?"

"Yes. Yes, of course we will. And Margaret?"

"What?"

"Paul is going to visit Nora soon. I'm asking you to let Nora take care of herself when he comes, okay? The nurse will be right outside the door. And I am only a phone call away. Can you do that?"

She nods her head up and down, vigorously.

"You have done an amazing job. You are just like St. Margaret in the story. You have slain the dragon with your sword."

She is feeling proud. She will ask him a big question.

"Before I go, will you . . . will you . . . will you give me a goodnight kiss on my forehead?"

"Oh, Margaret, yes, of course."

She wraps her arms around herself then, whispers goodbye, and closes her eyes.

David walks over, leans down, and kisses her on her forehead.

"Goodbye, brave Margaret. Sleep tight."

Nora awakens in the middle of the night. She thinks about her last conversation with David—him saying Margaret agreed to let her be in charge. Nora closed her eyes after he'd said this, and in the midst of all her relief she felt an immense sense of loss.

She switches on the night-light, reaches for a glass of water. There is the photograph, leaning against the glass. She picks it up. Her father had taken this picture the day she'd received the Valentine's dress from her grandmother. Taken the picture a week before he ruined the dress. Taken the picture when she'd been a good girl. And now—her father's mouth, breathing heavy in her ear, whispering, *If you tell you will be alone. All alone. No one will believe you. If you tell, no one will ever believe you.*

In her mind, suddenly, her own voice as a child:

"One, two, three, four, five, six, seven, eight, nine, ten. One, two, three, four, five, six, seven, eight, nine, ten. One, two, three, four, five, six, seven, eight, nine, ten . . ." Nora closes her eyes, and here is her six-year-old self in the classroom coat closet. The smell of wet boots and wool.

"Nora?"

It is Sister Rosa. "Nora, what are you doing here? You should be on the bus!"

"One, two, three, four, five, six, seven, eight, nine, ten. One, two, three, four, five, six, seven, eight, nine, ten. One, two, three, four, five, six, seven, eight, nine, ten. One, two, three, four, five, six, seven, eight, nine, ten. One, two, three, four, five, six, seven, eight, nine, ten. One, two, three, four, five, six, seven, eight, nine, ten . . ."

Sister Rosa kneeling down, touching her knee. "Nora?"

Silence.

"Nora, what's wrong? Please tell me."

Tell her. She will help us. Tell her. "I . . . I . . . can't go home."

"Why not?"

Tell her.

"Nora, forgive me, but I have to call your mother."

No, no, no. Not our mother. She will kill us. Her eyes flash wide.

"It'll be all right. I'll be right back."

"Wait," Nora says through chattering teeth. "Will . . . will . . . you take me home?"

"Of course," and then, even softer, "of course."

In the car, Sister Rosa says, "Nora, we've known each other for a few years now."

"Yes, Sister. Since first grade."

"And we've prayed many, many times together."

"Yes, Sister."

"Can you please tell me what's wrong?"

Tell her.

"Do you still pray to St. Margaret?"

She closes her eyes. She is so sleepy.

"Nora? Do you still pray to St. Margaret?"

"Yes, Sister."

"And she's kept you safe."

Tell her.

When Sister Rosa stops the car in the Bauers' driveway, she turns to Nora and takes her hands into her own. "You're not alone," she says and closes her eyes. Breathes deep, folds her hands into prayer. "Saint Margaret," she says fiercely. "Hear me. See this beautiful girl. Protect her, now and forever. Amen."

"Amen," Nora whispers.

Maeve opens the door in her stocking feet and says, "Sister Rosa," in a startled, slurred voice. It's 4:00 in the afternoon, and Nora knows she's been drinking for at least an hour. Auburn hair loose and messy, nervousness sparks from her glassy eyes as she looks at the nun, her daughter, and back again to the nun. A nun has never visited the house before. Maeve is wearing a wrinkled blouse with stains down the front and self-consciously crosses her arms over her chest. Nora averts her gaze, doesn't dare make eye contact, looks at her shoes. Ears burning.

Sister Rosa holds Nora's hand tight. "Mrs. Bauer, Nora was helping me with a project, and somehow the time got away from us, and she missed the bus. I hope that hasn't caused a problem." Her words an icy river.

"Of course not," Maeve says, and Nora knows she is being careful to pronounce her words. "It was so nice of you to bring her home." And she is saying things a good mother might say. "Would you like to come in? It's freezing out there."

"No, thank you. I need to get back." Sister Rosa drops Nora's hand. Her eyes, soft and deep with protection, meet Nora's. "I'll see you tomorrow."

"Yes, Sister." *Please don't leave us here.*

"Goodbye, Mrs. Bauer. You have a very special young woman here." When Maeve says nothing, only smiles tightly, Sister Rosa says, meeting Maeve's eyes straight on with the intensity of someone threatening battle, "But I'm sure you know that."

Nora follows her mother through the doorway, and the door clunks closed. Her mother walks to the coffee table and picks up her glass of gin, takes a drink, the green olive touching her lips, then floating around the clear liquid again. She slams the glass back down. "What did you say to her?"

"Nothing." Nora steps back.

"You told her something."

Fear shakes Nora's body, and her skin pales. "No . . . no . . . Mommy."

"Didn't you?" her mother says, coming closer.

Shivering all over.

Hard furious terrified woman hand bones against girlface-girlarm-girlback-girlbones. Again and again and again.

"You stupid girl! You've shamed us! Shamed us!" She stops, gulps more gin and Nora crawls away fast and slips downstairs to her piano.

A howl down the hall startles Nora into the present. The disinfectant smell of the hospital suddenly magnified, a monster pushing into her skin, her lungs, her throat until she gasps, sucks in enough air to breathe again. Again, the howl down the hall. Dark rises within her. Rises and swells. Rises and gathers force and becomes fire becomes blood becomes sound and the sound forces her body out of the bed and she begins running around and around the room arms and anger flailing pounding on walls and doors mouth open wide open wide and something fierce and violent rips open her heart rips her body open until she is not a woman not a girl only a screaming mouth a screaming heart a screaming body.

CHAPTER TWENTY-SEVEN
FEBRUARY 13, 1997

Nora wakes to the familiar fog of residual drugs. *Shit. Now what?* And in the haze: *How much more can I take until I'm planted in a wheelchair, staring at the same spot on the floor all day, eyes flat as stamps, murmuring silvery syllables that slip away like fish into an unfathomable ocean?*

"Good morning." It's David. "I heard about last night," he says, taking off his coat. He pulls up a chair to the bed.

This can't be good. She reaches a drugged hand for her notebook, her pen.

"Nora. Wait."

She waits. Grateful to close her eyes again.

"You don't need to write. Just nod." Pause. "Do you remember anything after I left? Carol says you were holding the photo of yourself as a child."

She keeps her eyes closed and becomes acutely aware of the opaque mass that has invaded her brain cells, making it hard to concentrate, but then, there it is—the photo and Sister Rosa discovering her in the coat closet. Bringing her home. Her mother's anger. The secrets. The shame. The slam, slam, slam of the hand. Her father's mouth—*If you tell you will be alone. No one will ever believe you.*

The scream.

"Oh!" she says, and opens her eyes.

"Your voice is back!"

She sinks into the bed, closes her eyes, inhales, holds the air for a moment, stunned, nervous the sounds might be temporary, then through sheer force of will, clears her throat and pushes out another "Oh." The sound bursts forth, shimmering and clear. She smiles uneasily.

"Keep going," David says softly.

"Ahhhhhhh," she says then, her body softening. "Ah, ah, ah, ah, ah, ah, ah, ah," up and down the C scale, slowly at first, then a bit faster, then loud and soft, over and over again, trying to get the breathing right, each sound giving her more confidence, more energy, reassuring her she's lived through the hardest parts, she's moving forward. And now she hums random notes, as if she is walking home from school on a pleasant day, the sounds still shy, as if they are surprised to represent her and her alone.

"Open your eyes, Nora," David says. "Open your eyes."

She opens her eyes. Blinks at the cool white of the tamper-proof ceiling lamp. "I . . . I . . ." she whispers, and then more loudly, "I'm going home." She bolts up, turns to David, says in a faint but unwavering voice, "I'm going home. Today."

He looks stricken. "Getting your voice back is tremendous. And—" he collects himself, leans forward, says calmly, "and you must give this time. There's so much we haven't processed." He pauses. "We need to talk about the scream, how you felt about it, how you feel about having your voice back, how you feel about Margaret. There's just—we should talk about these things." He stands up. Walks to the window, shoves his hands in his pockets, stares out. "And . . ."

"And what?"

He turns to her, and she can see him try to keep his face neutral. "Tomorrow—tomorrow is, well, it's Valentine's Day."

She'd lost track of the days. She can see how such a thing might happen in a place like this, a place where all you can do is crawl over and across your mind, crawl in circles arguing with yourself, confuse your feelings, try to figure out what went wrong, crawl into hiding only to have someone pull you out and force you to take side-trips and tie your feelings into knots and then pull on threads. A place where all you can do is look down the hall and at the ceiling and out the window and make everything a metaphor. And yet, (maybe because of this) she believes that *now* she can handle it. *It* being Valentine's Day. Something more than her voice has been returned to her, and she knows she can rise above *it*.

"I can handle it," she says softly, as if she doesn't want to scare the words away. "I'm ready to go home, to start again."

David sighs. "I understand, but I can't sign you out today." He pauses and looks out the window, his breath making a foggy patch. "I won't. I'm sorry, but this is too rushed." He turns to look at her. "You have to be sure, Nora. You are strong. But you have to be sure."

"You think I'll run out into the street again," her voice narrow and watery. "Throw myself through a window."

"I just suggest you have at least one visit with Paul, Fiona, and James like you planned," he says. "Then see. If all goes well, we can talk about you going home, create an outpatient schedule—"

"I don't need you to sign me out," she whispers. "I'm a voluntary patient, and I can leave whenever the hell I want."

"Nora," he says in a weary voice. "Voluntary or not, there's a process that must be followed. You *cannot* simply sign yourself out. If Dr. Brinkley and I feel you might be a danger to yourself or others, as much as we'd hate to do it, we'd get a court order. He pauses, inhales, exhales slowly. "Being *committed* is, well, once you're committed, it's much more difficult to get out." His large fingers shove hard through his white hair. "That's the reality."

Silence except for metal carts clanking down the hall. Silence except for the whine of country music floating slow in the background and an occasional muffled cry or scream. She feels like a child. Elation drained out of her. She leans back, exhausted, fights anger, says slowly, "How *sure* do I have to be, do *you* have to be, for me to get the hell out of here? How *complete* does the healing have to be?"

"Nora, we've talked about this. There's no such thing as *complete* healing." His ears, neck reddening. He walks to the nightstand, grabs a water glass, and heads for the bathroom. She hears him fill the glass. Guzzle the water. Now he stands in the doorway, says, "This is—"

"What? This is what?"

"It's lifelong work, Nora. Lifelong. Look, when your feelings stabilize—"

"I'd like to call John," she says abruptly, a sudden panic rushing through her. A need for an outside ally, another solution. "I want to ask him to visit tomorrow." She's a bit breathless now and pauses to calm down, doesn't want to lose her new voice. "Will you at least sign off for that? Make sure he's on the okayed-visitors list?"

"John?" he says. "The principal of your school?"

"Yes."

He arches his brows again, rubs his forehead, but before he can say anything else, she says, "And I want to see him alone. Without you or a nurse or Dr. Brinkley. Seeing him will . . ." but she doesn't finish the sentence because she doesn't know what seeing him will mean. She just has the need to see him and prove she can handle things. She wants to test herself. "The nurses will be in the hall anyway, right?"

When he frowns, she says, "Look, if something goes wrong I'll stay another few weeks, okay? I promise."

CHAPTER TWENTY-EIGHT
FEBRUARY 14, 1997

She sits by the window. Below her, a line of people board a city bus one by one. Their faces, out of focus, make her heart fold inward, and she quickly looks past them between the buildings to the Puget Sound. A subdued blue sky darkened by clouds.

"Nora?" And now, John.

He holds a bouquet of yellow roses in one hand and a small book with a red ribbon around it in the other. His face ramshackle and open like an old house. For a moment, she feels like they're on the set of a play and she's become flustered and forgotten her lines, but then she remembers.

"Hi," she says and stands and walks toward him. She is wearing her red socks because they seem festive, and she doesn't want to be reminded that her running shoes don't have laces.

"Hello," he says, a bit formally, and she thinks the nurses have told him that whatever he does, he shouldn't mention *what day it is.*

So she says it. This is, after all, a test. "Happy Valentine's Day." She waits to see if something bad will happen, if Margaret will come out, but she only feels herself standing there, and the lightness of her singular weight both startles and thrills her. Maybe Margaret will keep her promise. Maybe she's exhausted her purpose.

"It's good to see you," he says, presenting her with the roses.

She arranges the flowers in a plastic glass on her nightstand. "Beautiful," she says, heart pulsing nervously.

He hands her the book he brought. *The Book of Light* by Lucille Clifton.

"Thank you. She's one of my favorite poets—but I don't have this collection."

He hugs her then. It surprises her that she puts her cheek on his coat. After a few moments, she steps back, blushing, and it's hard to know what to say.

"Shall we sit?" he says, motioning to the chairs. He walks over to the same chair David usually sits in—the one by the window. She settles into the one opposite him, the book on her lap. She stares at it momentarily as if she might untie the ribbon, but she is really just trying to find words.

"This is weird, isn't it?"

He unbuttons his raincoat, leans over, and takes her hands in his. "People go through shit. You're just taking care of things, trying to make things better. That's all that matters, right? That we try to make things better?" He is wearing a green flannel shirt, a shirt you might wear on an easy Sunday while you read the *Times* and listen to Etta James. The image relaxes her. His words relax her. Things *will* be better from now on. She knows it. She will leave this place, move into an apartment with Fiona, and get back to teaching. Get back to her life.

For an hour, they talk. He tells her funny stories about the kids at school, and she nods and laughs. He tells her how much her students miss her, and she asks questions about the ones she knows he keeps his eye on. They talk about Elizabeth. She sets the book on the windowsill then, and begins to cry. He pulls her to her feet and holds her and walks her to the bed and they sit on the edge of it, arms wrapped around each other, her head on the rise and fall of his chest, and they say nothing at all.

When it's time to go, he asks if she needs anything, asks if she'll call him tomorrow. She says no, she doesn't need anything, and yes, she'll call. He kisses her on the cheek, and she actually wants more and tilts her mouth up. But then she is on a stage again, and Billie Holiday is singing "All of Me," and the whole thing feels so corny she bursts out laughing. And suddenly, Carol is there asking, "Are you alright? Are you okay?"

"Fine," John says, laughing too, and because he says that—*"Fine"*—even though he doesn't know why she is laughing, it is like being transported into normal.

"Bye," he says to her with a boyish wave

when it's time to go. "I look forward to talking tomorrow."

"Me too."

Once he's gone, she picks up *The Book of Light* and unties the red ribbon. Lets it float to the bed. She sits in the chair by the window. Stares at the cover of the book. There's a woman, not old, not young, with green hair, head bowed, eyes closed. Near the woman's head, a blue-green light in dark space. *A revelation? A hole in the sky?* Nora opens the book to the first page. An inscription: YOU ARE NOT ALONE. WITH YOU ALWAYS. JOHN. Her finger traces his words. She smiles, turns the page. Synonyms for light, stream-sparkle-flicker-spark-fire-blaze, radiate off the page and saturate her skin. She reads the words over and over and over again. She's made it through Valentine's Day.

CHAPTER TWENTY-NINE
FEBRUARY 17, 1997

It's been five days since the scream, since she's had her voice back, and for the first time in thirty years, she feels her voice is hers alone. She sits on a green vinyl couch in the visitor's room, waiting for Paul. The room, with its vague gray paint, everything stale and smelling of ammonia, isn't much better than her private room, but at least there isn't a hospital bed with its insinuation of vulnerability and disorder. And she'd asked that Paul visit in the early afternoon when most of the patients stop screaming and take naps. She wants to reassure him she is not crazy. Her visit with John proved she was stronger, and if she can manage Paul, she knows David and Dr. Brinkley will sign her release papers. She'd brushed her hair, applied lipstick. Smiled at herself in the mirror. *I'm ready.*

There are only three other people in the room. One person is Carol. She sits in a metal chair by the door, knitting. She is there to make sure things don't get out of control. The other two people are an old man and an old woman. They sit together on an orange vinyl couch over by the window. The old woman stays in room 404, two doors down from Nora's room. Nora has seen her rocking in a chair by the window, heard her make low moaning sounds at night. Sometimes the old man sits by her bed and reads to the old woman from the newspaper. Sometimes he holds her hands, kisses her pale lips, and brushes the limp gray hair from her face.

Nora thinks then about the first time Paul said, "I love you." They were sitting at a greasy linoleum table in Spud's Fish and Chips at Alki Beach, sipping vanilla milkshakes and dipping french fries in ketchup. "I love you," he'd said, holding a fry to her lips, and she'd opened her eyes wide. They'd known each other less than a year, and she knew he liked to date around, liked to keep things "uncomplicated"—keep his options open.

She'd chewed up the french fry, tried to swallow it, but it seemed to swell in her throat, her tongue thick with salt, and she had to gulp her milkshake in order not to choke. She licked her lips, almost said, "Why?" but ended up saying nothing at all because she didn't know what to say. She knew she should say, "I love you," back, but she couldn't because what did she know about love? She'd never been in love before, never felt the way the women in books and movies seemed to feel when they were in love, and she didn't feel that way now. Or at least she didn't think she did. It was hard to know.

"Did you hear me?" he'd asked, slightly embarrassed.

"Yes, yes, I did. Sorry."

"Am I too prosaic for you? Too commercial?"

He was always asking her this. Always wondering if they were a good fit because she loved poetry and he hated it, except for the rhyming kind.

"Am I," he'd said again. "Am I too staid for you?"

She shrugged, ate another fry.

"I could try and be a poet, but I'd probably blow it," he said.

She laughed, fed him a fry. Let him lick the salt from her fingers.

"You're different than the others," he'd said then.

She squirted some ketchup onto her plate, swirled a french fry around in it, and ate it.

"You don't care about a lot of things most women waste time over—you know, like clothes and jewelry and hair," he said. "You're beautiful—in a really natural way." And she'd thought then of that tampon commercial, that one with the make-up free girl hiking up a mountain even though she was having her period. *Tampons for the all-natural, adventurous woman.* She'd never felt natural like that woman. She'd never felt natural at all.

"And as long as we've known each other," he said, "I've never seen you freak out over stupid little things—you know, like if I'm a few minutes late or something—I've never seen you freak out at all." He'd emptied his milkshake, wiped his mouth on his sleeve. "I like that about you. I really do."

They'd looked at each other for a long moment before he said, "I shouldn't have said something so important in a fish-and-chips dive. Shit, I'm sorry." He'd taken her hand, wiped a bit of ketchup off her finger with a napkin. "I'll say it again later. Somewhere romantic, okay?"

And several weeks later, during a candlelight dinner at his apartment, Pachelbel playing on the stereo, he'd said it again, gazing at her, his face soft with affection, and she'd said it back to him. She'd felt a strong affection for him in that moment, an affection that might have been love. Sitting together like that with champagne and caviar, all on a white tablecloth, it *did* feel like a scene in a movie, and for the first time that she remembered, she'd felt normal, she'd felt hope that she was normal. Also, she thought it might be nice to be with someone.

"Nora?"

It's Paul. He stands there. He looks handsome. He's wearing a down jacket she hasn't seen before, and jeans instead of khakis. She rises to her feet, uncertain, says a slightly embarrassed hello. She realizes he will see her differently now. And she's right. His face is a mixture of shock and sympathy. Has she changed that much? She knows her weight has dropped, she's felt the sunken space between her hipbones, but she made an effort this morning to put on make-up and change out of her robe into a T-shirt and jeans.

"How are you?" he says, walking over to her. Close up, she can see the bags under his eyes, the dark circles of exhaustion.

"Better. I'm better."

They sit down, stiff and awkward on the green vinyl couch. Uncomfortable silence.

"You have your voice back," he says.

"Yeah."

"And you made it through Valentine's Day?"

"Yes," she says, blushing, thinking about John. Then, "Is Fiona okay?"

"She's okay, but she's worried about you. Asks about you all day. We've told her you're getting better, that you were just really tired and needed a rest." He crosses his arms, hands dig into armpits. "God, what you've been through."

"I'm better." Her eyes sting and she doesn't know what else to say. She doesn't want to say the wrong thing. He is acting so careful.

He tells her he's sorry he hasn't visited, explains how he'd been nervous to—that he might have made things worse, might have undone the work she was doing here. And then he says, a darkness passing over his face, his voice thick with pain, "Did you really think I could hurt Fiona?"

"I didn't—"

"But you did. Dr. Forrester said that a part of you—Margaret," he stops for a moment, looks down, looks so embarrassed that a flash of humiliation rips through Nora's chest. A normal man sitting with a crazy woman in a psych ward. He meets her eyes again. His eyes wet with tears. "Margaret said that I . . . I . . . might have hurt Fiona."

"But did he tell you why—that she doesn't trust *any* men," Nora swallows, then adds, "except for him."

"But she's *you,* right? She *is* you. So at some level, *you* thought I could hurt our daughter."

She wants a pillow to clutch, but there isn't one. Her hands tremble so badly she sits on them. She is frightened by her shame, ashamed of her accusations. She doesn't want to float away.

Carol issues a warning cough, glares at Paul, asks, "Everything okay?"

"Fine," Nora says. Carol's voice is an anchor, reminding her how badly she wants to go home. She moves her hands to her lap. Folds them. They are still trembling, but once they are folded together, it isn't as noticeable. *Breathe in calm, breathe out reason. You can do this.*

"Nora?"

She opens her eyes. *When had she closed them?* Here are his dark eyes, sad as the winter sky. None of this is his fault.

"Paul, I'm sorry. Please forgive me. I know you wouldn't hurt Fiona." She exhales deeply. "I know you wouldn't."

"I wouldn't. God, of course I wouldn't."

"I'm sorry."

"Time's up," Carol says.

"Did you ever love me?" he says.

She says nothing. She thinks again, about the night with the candlelight. How afterward they'd gone into his bed. He'd read a poem to her, one he'd written himself, holding the loose paper in his hands, vulnerable, intimate. But vaguely, she'd known her body didn't hold the passion it should have, that she hadn't wanted to melt into his bones, hadn't wanted the lights on, had wanted it dark. She'd drifted into some other space in her mind, when he'd pressed then pushed into her, that she'd been grateful when he'd finally rolled off her body. And how, despite the fact she'd lost concentration and he'd fallen asleep without saying anything, she'd felt content to lie there with him, body touching body. Content enough to marry him. Relieved she would no longer be alone.

The old man by the window stands and pulls the blinds open. An enormous shaft of light beams into the room, and the old woman claps her hands and laughs. The old man laughs too.

"Nora, do you—did you love me?"

"I-I don't know. Maybe. I don't know. I've

been really messed up. Sorry, I don't know. In the beginning, I thought so, and then—I don't know."

"I know you've been through a lot," he says, casting a glance at Carol, who is watching closely. His voice softens. "Jesus. I'm really sorry about all of it, really I am. But . . . I think . . . I need to . . . I need to . . . to leave *us*."

"Elisa," she says, looking at her hands.

He is quiet for several moments. "Yes."

"You've taken off your ring," she says.

"Yes. And yours?"

"They took it." She lifts a shoulder toward Carol. "For now. They took my shoelaces too." Now she is crying. Fifteen years of marriage. Over. Done. No more.

He leans over, hugs her hard.

"I'm okay," she whispers into his ear. "I'm okay."

"Don't rush this. Please. Don't rush coming home," he says, handing her a Kleenex from a box on the end table and taking one for himself.

"But Fiona . . ."

"You'll see her tomorrow, right? James too?"

She wipes her eyes. "Yes."

He stands, kisses the top of her head, and like that, they are no longer together.

CHAPTER THIRTY
FEBRUARY 18, 1997

"Mommy!" Her daughter races toward her. Nora kneels, wraps up Fiona, pulls her close, smells the love and light and strength of her. Fiona whispers into her ear. "I missed you so much! Are you okay? When are you coming home?"

"Soon, honey. Very soon." She stands to hug James, Fiona latched onto her leg. He looks terrible. Bloodshot eyes, the lines in his forehead deepened.

"Nice digs," he says, gazing around the visitor's room, gingerly returning her hug. "The ribs doing better?"

"Yes, yes, better."

A teenage girl wrapped in a crocheted throw comes in then, and for a moment, Nora thinks it is Elizabeth, but of course, it is not. The girl has short purple hair and pale white skin. Multiple eyebrow piercings over her left eye. She glances at them and trudges to the snack table. She pours coffee into a Styrofoam cup, rips open a yellow packet of sweetener, and lets it snow slowly into the coffee, then walks to one of the five vinyl-covered loungers in front of the TV and slumps there, stares at it without turning it on.

"Who's that, Mommy?"

"I don't know." It disturbs Nora then to realize that in all this time, she hasn't spoken to any of the patients. For twelve days she hasn't done anything but work with "the team," sit and stare out the window and manage the delicate space between thinking too much and not at all, walk the halls to keep her blood flowing, eat (Carol sitting there every few hours, insisting she swallow something, threatening an IV if she doesn't), vomit, pee, sleep, take an occasional shower (the shower only because Carol puts her in, waits outside while Nora cries inside) . . . except for today.

Today in the shower, Nora's body wet, the sensation of water, the sound and clean of it sinking into her skin, rippling over her breasts, a reuniting of her face with her arms, chest, legs and feet, skin and bones. It might as well have been the entire sea washing over her, her sense of self that real.

Fiona's voice brings her back. "Oh! Look! Can I draw something?" At the far end of the room an easel stands holding a giant sketch pad.

"Of course, but give me one more big hug!"

Fiona hugs Nora hard, says, "I love you so much, Mommy!" and then runs to the easel. Nora and James sit down in restrained emotion and watch as Fiona chooses a yellow crayon and draws a huge flower. Next, Fiona replaces the yellow crayon with a green one and draws a stem for the flower.

"Paul says she's okay."

"She is—but God, she really misses you."

Nora keeps her eyes on her daughter. "I miss her too. More than anyone can know." Above her, from the speakers, Garth Brooks drawls out "Friends in Low Places."

"Your psychiatrist suggested we not say too much to her for now, said you would talk with her once you're home, said the most important thing is she knows she's not to blame."

She turns to him, tries to ignore the music. *Seriously. Who would play that in a psych ward?* "Thank you for being here with her. I know it's a lot to be away from Stephen—"

"Stephen's fine," he says, takes her hands in his. "But I'm so . . . so . . . outraged about Dad— I . . . I can't—" he chokes on his words, hands clench, practically crush their bones into fists.

"James."

"Damn him," he whispers, each word convulsing. "Damn the son of a bitch. Nora, he hired an investigator to find us! He's known where we lived for months and he never said a word! Only sent that damn Christmas box. Jesus. And then when I told him what you remembered—"

His words slam hard as an iron pipe. Things are going wrong. "You told him?" She goes white and yanks her hands from his. "Oh, my God! You shouldn't have done that! What if . . . what if he comes after me? What—"

"Nora! Stop! Please! He is a frail, old man with dementia. He's in a nursing home with locked doors. Half the time I visit he doesn't even know me. He can barely leave his chair. He's not going anywhere. And even if he could, none of us would let him anywhere near you. God, I'm sorry. I shouldn't have said anything."

She twists her body away from him and turns to Fiona who is drawing a purple bird next to the yellow flower. She inhales and exhales and her hands drop onto her lap, the fingers lace tightly together. Without moving her head, she says, "What did he say? When you told him, what did he say?"

James is silent. She braces herself. At last he says, "He denied it. The bastard denied it all."

She feels a fist of anger in her chest, but still, she is okay. She's not going to let him ruin her life anymore. She's not. She can't. She wants to get out of here. She turns to James. "And you?"

"Nora, I believe you," he says, his eyes welling. "I believe you."

She is unprepared for the force of this sentence. A wall breaks apart inside her.

"Thank you," she says.

"And I'm so sorry I wasn't here for you more. I'm really sorry. I just didn't know. Why didn't you tell me?" he says.

"I . . . I didn't know. I—"

"Shame's in our veins, that's why," he says.

She knows these words. They're hers. Years ago, when he was sixteen, she'd seen him and an older boy kissing out behind the garage. After dinner, she'd gone into James' bedroom and asked him about it. He'd sat on the bed, put his head in his hands and said, *"Shit, shit, shit."* She'd promised she wouldn't tell. No one would understand, she'd known that. Still, she'd said, "Hold your head high, James. Don't let shame poison your veins. You're perfect. Absolutely perfect, and I love you."

"James, I think the weight, the weight that's pushed me down for the last thirty years is lifting. I know I've got a long way to go. Every time I think of him, I . . . I hurt, hurt in places I didn't know existed, in ways I—but still . . . I can't—"

He pulls her tighter into him. "Fuck him. You don't owe him a thing. You never have to see him again. This isn't about him anymore, do you understand? This is about you getting better. This is about us doing whatever it takes to bring you home."

They sit for a while, her head against the tremble of his chest. The inflating and deflating of his lungs coaxing a delicate part of her to life.

"Nora, I—"

"What?"

"No, never mind. It's nothing. Sorry."

"What? Tell me. I can handle it. Really."

"Paul . . . he isn't at the house very often. He's home for dinner, tucks Fiona into bed. We've hardly said two words. I think he's . . . staying with—"

"Elisa. Yes, I know." She is surprised how remarkably calm she feels saying this. "He was here yesterday. Paul and I are done."

His arm squeezes her shoulders. "Well, I'm staying. For as long as you need me."

"Mommy," Fiona calls from across the room. "Can you help me tear off this picture?"

Nora rises, makes herself walk steadily to her daughter. Fiona has drawn a purple hummingbird, its long beak deep into the sweetness of a yellow daffodil.

"Sweetie, this is beautiful."

"My teacher says the daffodil is a symbol of new life, and the hummingbird is a symbol of happiness."

Nora ruffles her hair. "Well you are a very smart little girl—and a wonderful artist."

"A symbol is something that gives you a clue of something," Fiona says proudly. "Like red is a clue for love. That's why valentines are red."

Nora's stomach constricts.

"And you can make symbols from everything! Did you know that Mommy? And you can think of the symbol whenever you want. That's what the teacher told me. She said I can think of a hummingbird, and I will feel better."

"And do you think of the hummingbird?"

"Yes!" Fiona says. "All the time! And I make symbols out of lots of things. Ask me to make a symbol from something, Mommy."

"Well," Nora says, her stomach relaxing a bit, "what's James a symbol of?"

They both look at him. He smiles and waves.

Fiona puts her hands on her hips. "That's too easy! James is a symbol of love! Give me something harder."

"Well, how about a TV?"

Fiona is quiet for a moment. Looks at the TV and then at the girl.

"Hmmm," she says. "That . . . that is a symbol for a friend. Maybe also, lonely." She adds a bit more purple to each hummingbird wing, and stands back to inspect it. "It's perfect. Mommy, can you get me the picture down?"

Nora carefully tears the drawing from the binding, gives it to Fiona. Fiona runs to the girl in front of the TV and offers her the picture.

The girl sets her Styrofoam cup on a side table and raises her hands slowly to take the gift.

Nora walks back to sit with James, keeps her eyes on her daughter, sees the young woman hold the picture up and study it carefully and then set it on her lap. Fiona gives the girl a big smile and runs back to her mother.

"She liked it, Mommy!"

"That was lovely of you, honey."

Fiona clambers up on Nora's lap and nestles her head under her mother's chin. "But Mommy, that girl didn't talk at all. And her eyes were really sad." She wraps an arm across Nora. "But I could tell she liked it because of the way she touched the hummingbird's wings." Fiona reaches up and strokes Nora's cheek. "Like this."

Nora squeezes her. "Hey! I've been waiting for days to hear about your Valentine's party!" Fiona's body tightens. James clears his throat. "It's all right," Nora says. "We can talk about it." She isn't sure at all if it *is* all right, but she feels very hopeful.

She tilts Fiona's face up so she can look her in the eyes. "Honey, I'm really sorry for scaring you when you were sorting your candy. Really." Fiona's eyes well up. "And when I get home, we can talk more about why that happened, okay? But for now, let's just be happy, like hummingbirds!" Fiona blinks away tears, giggles, relaxes. "So please," Nora says, "tell me about your party. Did you get all your cards made?"

And Fiona tells her about each paper heart she'd made, each note she'd written, how she carefully taped a candy heart to each red envelope. And, at first, in between Fiona's words, Nora remembers to breathe, she's fine. But now, a slight quickening of her heart, and when Fiona begins to recite the words on each heart, *"I like you!" and "You're fun!" and "Kiss me!"*

Nora begins to slip
the sweetened words
undressing her
the weightlessness before
her father heavy on
her stillness
and she raises her hips
the floating up,
stay here, stay here,
Fiona's voice deep underwater,
she begs Margaret in the most fierce way—
"Nora!" Carol's voice. Carol shaking, shaking, shaking her.

Eyes open. Fiona there, red cheeks wet, her little hand over her mouth, James' eyes wet too, and the girl with the crocheted blanket holding the hummingbird picture staring, everyone blinking alarm.

"Mr. Bauer," Carol says, "How about taking the little one out?"

"Mommy," Fiona says then, in a tiny forlorn voice, but all Margaret can do is shut her eyes tight.

CHAPTER THIRTY-ONE
FEBRUARY 20, 1997

Nora lies in bed listening to Carol whisper, "—and she kept screaming, *'Let me go home. Let me go home,'* in a child's voice, so out of control—a code gray—five aides to subdue her, scared the hell out of her little one. And ever since then, oh God, the screaming. You'd think she was coming off heroin or something, even broke one of the aides' fingers!"

And then, another woman's voice: "Her husband's getting the court involved—wants her moved to Woodhaven."

Nora waits until they are gone before she rises from the bed. It takes her a few minutes—the medication makes it hard to think straight. She takes her red wool coat from its hanger and her sweater and jeans from the chest of drawers and lays them on the bed. She pulls off her nightgown and gets dressed, pulls on her socks and running shoes. The missing laces make her cringe, make her burn. Her heart thumping shame. She'd let Fiona talk about the hearts, believed she could handle it, but she couldn't. Why had she felt so much better earlier, only to have Margaret fracture her again? Her brain is ruined, and now she knows this. Broken. Irreparable.

She rips a piece of paper out of her notebook, but they've taken the pen, so she writes clumsily with lipstick, writes with an aching shame, *Fiona, I love you.* Tears the paper into the shape of a heart and leaves it by the yellow roses, puts on her coat, and tiptoes to the doorway. Looks both ways. No one. She slips out and closes the door behind her and whisper-walks down the aqua-tiled corridor to the public phone booth near the exit. She hears voices and presses herself into the booth, holds her breath, and waits. Finally, here is the janitor with his rattling cart and jangly keys, unlocking the metal bar across the door. He pushes it open, and once he's clanked through, she rushes over and jams her foot into the opening. His sounds fade and she runs down the hall and out the double doors.

It is dark and the cold stings her face. The sidewalks are illuminated by streetlamps, the yellowish glare making her feel like she's on a stage, and she has to stop for a moment to regain her balance. But then she runs, runs several blocks down sloping sidewalks to the water. People lying bundled in the *Seattle Times* in doorways littered with butts and rubbish. She keeps her eyes down when the drunks and junkies stumble by. Yellow taxis speed and stop, buses lurch into curbs, suddenly enormous, their pneumatic doors hiss, their filthy pipes spew exhaust into her face and she keeps running, and now here are the cathedral bells ringing five o'clock and she can't think about how Fiona loves those bells she can't think about Fiona, it's for the best, it's for the best, it's for the best.

Once she arrives at the waterfront she slows, breathing hard, walks between run-down warehouses to an abandoned pier. Gulls keening overhead. High tide. Waves pulse loud, slap against pilings; a sudden penetrating smell of creosote and seaweed. The rough wooden planks creak under her feet. She arrives at the end and wraps her arms around herself and looks across the blue swells to the mountains, shadows in the dim light of dawn. A ferry boat blows its horn.

She peers into the water and imagines herself diving into the blackness. Pulling herself down, down, down, mouth open drinking freedom swallowing loss lungs release forever emancipation beneath despair sinking somewhere holy.

Her arms raise and she bows her head, palms coming together like a prayer. Deep inhale. But then her grandfather's voice: *You are tough; you are stronger than you think. You are tough; you are stronger than you think* . . . and she hesitates.

In that moment, a cry. Child sounds. She holds her breath. Listens.

Silence.

She waits. Arms still raised. Again, a cry—from behind the dumpster. She brings her arms down. Walks numbly toward the sound.

Here is the sound.

A child. Her dress is red. Her eyes are blue. A little girl sits. Arms locked around exposed knees. Rocking. Blonde hair infused with light.

Here is Margaret.

Nora shakes her head, tries to shake off the numb, the disbelief of seeing her there. The incandescent skin and bones and eyes of her. The blue eyes. Nora steps closer, tentative with apprehension that any sudden movement might make her disappear. Margaret keeps rocking, rocking, rocking. They stare at each other. Blue meeting blue.

"Margaret?" Nora says.

"I . . . I . . . don't want to die," Margaret cries then, rubbing the sleeve of her blouse across her face, smearing tears across her cheeks. "Please. Please. Don't let us die, I-I-I've worked very, very hard."

"Margaret?" Nora whispers, whole body aching.

"I've barely, I've barely—" but then Margaret begins to cry again and buries her face in her hands.

Nora takes off her coat, hands shaking, and wraps it around Margaret's shoulders. Falls to her knees in front of her. Split suddenly open, inside out. The hero child is real. The hero child who arrived each time she was needed, who knew when to play dead.

"Margaret, I am . . . I am . . ."

Margaret stops rocking, says, "Am I no one?"

This question from six-year-old pink lips.

"No!" Nora says, though the second she says it she can taste the lie. Guilt fills her. She's hated, blamed, and denied Margaret. Used her. Wanted to drown her. Mother annihilating child. Nora draws in a breath, reaches, touches Margaret's face. Struggles for words that won't feel small and failing in her mouth, words true enough to bear the monster weight of this child's pain. This child's war-weariness. "I was wrong. I was so wrong," Nora says. When Margaret doesn't say anything, just keeps rocking, Nora says in a voice gaining strength, owning courage, "Listen to me, little warrior girl," the words aching in the back of her throat, "we are *not* ruined. We are beautiful—beautiful and sacred and we are never giving up." And when she says this, right there, out loud, she knows this to be true.

Margaret stares at her, weighing pain, weighing truth, weighing love, and then, eyes brimming soft, raises her arms. Nora gathers her tight, kisses her into her breast, absorbs more love than she's ever known. Margaret presses presses presses skin into bone into light into light into light into light into light into light.

ACKNOWLEDGMENTS

It would not have been possible to sustain the decade-long effort required to write this book without the constant support of many kind, generous, and loving people.

First, thank you to my sons, Ben and Roarke, my heaven and earth, who opened my heart in ways I hadn't known possible. I love you so much, and it is the greatest privilege to be your mother. Thank you to my stepson, Loren, who is a strong, beautiful force in our family, and has gifted us with a tremendous sense of humor and compassion.

To my husband, Peter, my touchstone, who gives me the kind of love I've never before experienced, who was my smartest first editor, who believes in me more than anyone I've ever known, who would hold both my hands each time I wanted to give up, and say, "This book is so important and beautiful and powerful."

Thank you to Laurence for his unwavering commitment to interior truth, his fearlessness in confronting it, and his willingness to shift the frame and ask, "Is there another way to think about this?"

I am grateful to all my editors and manuscript

readers: Dorothy Allison, Lidia Yuknavitch, Peggy Hageman, Marjorie Osterhout, Kate Kennedy, Karen Sullivan, Nancy Rekow, Sharon Dembro, Sylvia Bowman, Marcia Perlstein, Nyla Dartt, Courtney Vatis, and Gordon Warnock. Thank you for drawing out what I most struggled to express. Your brilliant, insightful questions expanded and deepened my story in a thousand ways.

To the crucible that is the Writers' Workshoppe & Imprint Books. Your astounding collective energy helped me grow me as a writer. Hands down. If it weren't for you, I wouldn't be the writer I am today.

And huge gratitude to the authors I've had the incredible honor to meet along the way, who offered fortifying advice and generous support: Rikki Ducornet, Dorothy Allison, Lidia Yuknavitch, Pam Houston, Melissa Febos, Sue William Silverman, Sonya Lea, Rene Denfeld, Sheila Bender, Susan Wooldridge, Erica Bauermeister, Jennie Shortridge, Adrianne Harun, Terry Persun, Bill Ransom, Cheryl Merrill, Julie Christine Johnson, Christine Fadden, and Louise Marley.

Thank you to my incredibly wonderful friends who encouraged and nourished me with love along the way: Karen, Maryann, Maggie, Carol, Holly, Bob, Helen, Sarah, Jason, Susan, and Tom.

This book would not exist without my brilliant, hardworking agent Gordon Warnock and the fabulous Blackstone team: Josh Stanton, Greg Boguslawski, Addi Black, Anne Fonteneau, Lauren Maturo, Jeffrey Yamaguchi, Peggy Hageman, Kathryn G. English, Josie McKenzie, Courtney Vatis, and Ananda Finwall.

Thank you to my tugboat, whose magic held me in solitude for hours on end as I wrote my heart out until the story was done.

Thank you to my sister, Eileen, who was there in ways no one else could ever know, in ways I've yet to find the words for.

And last but not least, to St. Margaret. I can still hear you.

Books are produced in the United States using U.S.-based materials

Books are printed using a revolutionary new process called THINKtech™ that lowers energy usage by 70% and increases overall quality

Books are durable and flexible because of smythe-sewing

Paper is sourced using environmentally responsible foresting methods and the paper is acid-free

Center Point Large Print
600 Brooks Road / PO Box 1
Thorndike, ME 04986-0001 USA

(207) 568-3717

US & Canada:
1 800 929-9108
www.centerpointlargeprint.com